THE UNSETTLING

by

Terri McEachren-Levert

Cover Art: Shelagh Dufour

Edited by: Jen Clarke

Library and Archives Canada catalogued this publication through Legal Deposit

McEachren-Levert, Terri L., 1971-, author
        The Unsettling/Terri McEachren-Levert

ISBN: 978-1-9992685-4-1

Published by: Reno Blue Productions, Chelmsford, ON P0M 1L0

Are you seated comfortably - curled up in a soft chair, or on a cozy couch? Or perhaps you're laying in bed, relaxed and warm?   Is there noise around you, like music or television in the background? Or are you in complete silence? Are you focused solely on the words you are reading on this page or are you distracted by something around you? Are your lights off? Are you alone?

If you don't like to be frightened or feel disconcerted, or if you are squeamish, perhaps this isn't the book for you. If your constitution is not strong, if you are not prepared for unexpected realities, and if you are disturbed easily by uncomfortable things, maybe you should close this book now and find something more gentle and to your liking.

But if you are prepared to be ill at ease and you enjoy your beliefs being challenged and your thoughts being confused, then settle in and steel yourself for an unnerving, unpleasant, and dare I say a creepy tale of what may or may not be real. Prepare yourself for ....

THE UNSETTLING

i:

"Uncle Lewis, there's a ghost in my closet!" I shout firmly with my proper British accent, stomping my foot on the worn, hardwood floor for emphasis, my black mary-janes clacking loudly.

As expected, in a moment he rushes into the room, albeit a little slower each time...he is tiring of this game. Only, it isn't a game...

"Adelia, you must stop shouting this nonsense."

He runs his hand through the feathery, coffee coloured locks that have fallen into his eyes, brushing the hair out of his face. He tries to sound angry, but the strictness in his voice tires towards the end. He looks at me with his hands on his hips, waiting.

"Well if you'd just show up when I called, you might see it next time." I throw my hands in the air and flop on the wooden, four poster bed. Laying on my stomach with the palms of my hands propping up my chin, I look back at him.

He goes towards the closet, to placate me by looking in. As his hand touches the doorknob, I flip over onto my back and gaze up at the ceiling with an exasperated sigh. I know he's humouring me. Frankly, it wouldn't matter whether he opened that door or not anyway.

"It's no use, he's gone now." I say, letting him off the hook, letting him continue existing in his world, as he'll never be able to see mine.

He pulls his hand away, and looks at me for a moment before sitting down beside me. I look up at him and he ruffles my hair, which I hate. I quickly sit up and smooth it back into place.

"You are a handful, little one," he mutters, shaking his

head.

Uncle Lewis is an even tempered man. Even though his height is average at best, he's still an imposing character. It is not size that makes the man, you see, it is the air about him – his personality, his attitude, the way he carries and conducts himself. I've never seen Uncle Lewis not wearing a suit and tie. He portrays himself as a man that is always in charge, always capable. He would never be able to fathom the idea that things occur beyond his control, things more powerful than even him.

"I just wish you'd believe me." I sigh loudly, picking imaginary fluff off my pleated black skirt.

"What I believe, is that you have a terrific imagination...and you like making me run from all over this huge house to see how fast I can make it to your room. Do you have a stopwatch?" he chuckles, looking out the large bay window which curves around to encompass the turret that is my bedroom. I follow his gaze.

The sun has gone down on Craymore Estate, setting gently

into the sea in it's nightly explosion of shades of pinks and oranges. My window seat, as well as the sitting room directly below my bedroom and the attic above, has the best view in the regal old Gothic Revival home. The view is breathtaking really, but I tire of it. It's begun to bore me. Sometimes I want to climb out my window onto the awning below and step off into that myriad of colours – whether it be the cerulean blues of the day sky, the aforementioned light show of dusk, or the purples and blacks of the night. I imagine being able to melt into the vibrant hues and become one with sky, ceasing to exist.

"But Uncle..." my voice trails into a hopeless whine.

"Get ready for bed, my dear. Morning comes early." He pats me on the head as he stands up. The sound of the heavy wooden door closing behind him echoes in the large empty house.

Such a huge home for a bachelor, inherited from his parents, who inherited it from theirs and so on and so forth. Many rooms, big and lonely, an entire wing not even used. Old furniture covered by sheets, untouched for years from a time where once the house was alive with people and parties. The glamour of the early years has long since faded, leaving only thick dust on heavy red and gold velvet curtains. From the few servants who remain I've heard tales of the home in it's prime, warm and animated, but I can't even imagine it. To me, it is just a lonely space that I share with my Uncle, since he took me in.

It was a terrible tragedy that brought me here, one that I don't really recall, even though I was part of it. My last memories are of laughing with my father as he ushered me into the backseat of the car, and singing with my mother right up until...well until it all goes black. I'm told it was a horrible crash. The spacious, black sedan had been smashed beyond recognition. We had been travelling to Craymore Estate as Father begrudgingly had business to take care of. I don't know that he ever said what it was. We were almost there, having driven for days, so close in fact,we were heading down the endless winding road which serpentined towards to the Estate. From what I remember, the singing stopped when my Mother saw something in the road and started to scream. I'll never know what it was.

The next thing I remember is waking up in the hospital, although I've thankfully forgotten most of that time. But amnesia is an expected consequence of a head injury as serious as mine, It was unknown how I even survived, with my brain swollen and my skull battered, but eventually I healed...well enough anyway. Uncle took me in and kept me to raise me as his own. Mother and Father were gone and I had nowhere else to go.

Uncle is well-meaning, but he does not know how to relate to a little girl, let alone raise a child. He only knows work and business, and carrying on the family legacy. My father was his only brother, and he had left the Estate, left the town of Ashby, long ago, ending up as far away as possible from his childhood home. I never knew what drove him away.

 As Uncle Lewis stays busy working out of his office study downstairs, locked up like Ebenezer Scrooge, the smell of cigars wafting from under the door, he leaves me to my own devices, my own entertainment. At first, I was dreadfully lonely. I'm only 13 years old after all. I need other people, stimulation, socialization. So, out of necessity really, I created my own imaginary friends...dolls and shadows who spoke to me. All well and good for a time..until they became real.

I tried to tell Uncle, in fact, I keep trying to tell him, but he never listens to me...he even began to worry about my sanity. Maybe my head injury caused irreparable harm, he pondered. Maybe I was traumatized more than he realized. Day after day, an ocean of time passed until I just accepted it as the norm.

With a breathy sigh, I roll my eyes, staring after my Uncle for a few moments. He will not believe me today either. I'll keep trying. It's all I can do.

Before I get into bed, I open the closet door and peer inside. My clothes, dresses, skirts and blouses of all colours hanging neatly from wooden hangers; the shelf above them filled with several pairs of shoes, both fancy dress and casual. The black figure, man-like in shape and appearance, hunkers in the corner of the closet, right

where he was when I called Uncle into my room. His
head turns and looks at me, a noose tightly around his
neck. His mouth opens in a silent scream; his neck flops
loosely to the side, bending at an impossible angle. I close
the door quietly. He'll be there again tomorrow.

ii:

I never felt quite right after the accident. A vague sense of
something being wrong, but nothing I could ever put my
finger on – some confusion, malaise, fatigue. I feel older
than my years, like my soul perished in the accident and
I'm left with an empty hole inside, a blank space where life
should be. A part of me is missing, the part that puts a
sparkle in your eye and emotion in your heart. The special
something that puts a lilt in your voice when you laugh, or
a spring in your step. The essence of who I was is gone,
and I feel like a stranger to my own self. It's frustrating to
try and put it into words, and I tire trying. Uncle calls it
grief...mourning. I don't know if it's as simple as that.

By far, the worst of the lingering effects of my crushed
skull continues to be frequent headaches. As usual, the

next morning I wake up with a dull ache. Sometimes it's a pounding or a throbbing deep inside my brain. It subsides after awhile, as long as I keep the curtains closed and lay very still. When it's at it's worst, a searing hot knife plunges into the deepest recesses of my head over and over again, and I pray to the entities in the home to take my pain away.

When I'm feeling better, I get dressed, choosing clothes from the large bureau across the room, so I don't have to open the closet today. I sit at the mirror and and gaze into my own eyes as I stroke my hair with the pearl handled brush that used to be my great grandmother's. It came with the vanity, a secret found inside it's drawers. Uncle told me this used to be her room.

I stare at my face, my scars, mostly but not totally, covered by my long, umber coloured hair – a jagged line travelling from my hairline down my cheekbone and ending at my right ear is the most obvious remnant of that night. I try to style my hair to hide it the best I can, but I'm always very aware of it's presence. It's like a branding, a disfigurement that screams at the world, 'Look what happened to me!'. My face reflects the wreckage that I was in; the wreckage that is now my life.

Putting the brush down, I continue staring into the mirror. Sometimes, if I concentrate hard enough, I see my Mother in my reflection, smiling warmly full of love. My Father might appear over my shoulder, his stern but proud face gazing upon me with encouragement. Today, however, the only thing I see, is a dark figure in the corner of the room behind me, partially hidden by the wardrobe. It crouches there watching me. It's head turns to follow me as I stand up and head towards the door. Looking back over my shoulder, I softly close it behind me.

The grand home with many rooms holds many secrets. It is to be expected when generations of family live within it's walls for hundreds of years. Successive people of all different temperaments, personalities, dreams and motives live, eat and sleep night after night, year after year... the house absorbs all their energy. The house becomes possessive and doesn't really like outsiders. I was an outsider when I arrived. Even though I am family. I wasn't raised here, I'd never been here. The house didn't know me. The gabled windows, like large, hooded eyes look at me suspiciously. I don't feel welcome here, not since day one.

We've come to an uneasy truce, this house and I. I accept the ghosts and shadows it sends to scare me as minor inconveniences, and it allows me to stay. They never show themselves to my Uncle, but perhaps he knows, albeit subconsciously, that they exist. He can probably feel his ancestors, his lost family members and maybe even their demons, existing just outside the continuum of his vision. Perhaps, in the corner of his eye, he catches a glimpse of movement, a shape that he convinces himself isn't there after all. But he can't accept it, so he blames it on my head injury, on my rambunctiousness, my youth...anything so he won't have to contemplate the possibility that it's real...and he drowns himself in work, because if he never looks up from his papers, he'll never come face to face with what's actually there.

Descending the grand staircase to the hallway, a large glass chandelier hangs high above my head. I'm always afraid it's going to let go and fall, crushing me, so my steps automatically quicken here. I can't understand how something so huge and heavy, adorned with jewels and lights can be suspended by a single cord. I gaze up at it in awe every time I pass under it, but only for a brief moment, lest I jinx it and send it crashing down on top of myself. At the bottom of the staircase are two intricately carved cherubs, one holding each banister. I usually avoid looking at them because their facial expressions never seem to be the same.

The dining room is filled with the smells of the morning meal cooking from the adjacent kitchen. Bacon, eggs and fresh baked bread overwhelm the scent of the enormous bouquet of red roses on the table in front of me. Miss Millie always makes sure an elaborate centrepiece adorns the dining table, changing with the seasons. Uncle has given her free reign to decorate as she sees fit, with no expense being spared. The clatter of pots, pans and dishes, as well as the staff talking amongst themselves makes the kitchen the only place in the house that ever sounds alive.

As usual, Uncle is not in the dining room when I sit at the large mahogany table to eat. He is always up at the crack of dawn and takes his coffee into his office, not to be seen for hours.   Upon hearing me take my seat, the butler emerges from the kitchen with a tray. He is an older gentleman, thin and tall. Balding, with a pronounced and crooked nose, he looks ever the epitome of a stereotypical English servant. He is professional and proper, always calm and serious. I've never known his name, and there's really no need for me to learn it. He gives a perfunctory smile, never meeting my eye, as he places my plate in front of me, precisely centred on the expensive linen place mat. A full English breakfast; far too much food for a little girl, but none of them are aware of the needs and habits of children. They can't be blamed for their ignorance, as they're just following orders from a well meaning, but clueless employer. Every morning, so much wasted food, yet huge portions are set before me day after day. It just serves to exemplify the impersonal and apathetic atmosphere I'm now a part of.

I pick at my plate. I never have much of an appetite; not since I've been here. It takes some getting used to – eating off the finest china, using the best crystal and fancy cutlery when it's not even a special occasion. We never lived like this when my parents were alive. How odd that my father would want to give up all these riches and luxuries to move across the country and live in relative squalor in comparison. What a dichotomy this life is. I am the product of two sides of a coin; two opposite and imposing factions which have now collided due to a terrible twist of fate.

The other 13 chairs are empty and I feel like a speck of dust in large, empty room. This house is always so quiet, as if ruminating on it's own thoughts. As a result, it leads me to do the same. No matter what room you are in, it is always just slightly too dark, and dare I even say gloomy, creating a vague feeling of discomfort and unease. The constant silence is deafening at times. I find myself longing for any sound, any noise, to take me out of my own head. The few staff that are left in the house keep themselves busy and while I can sometimes hear them murmuring, no one really engages with me. My feelings of being an outsider are reinforced, although I'm sure they mean well and are always pleasant. I am to be cared for, minded even... but their jobs do not include attachment or attentiveness. They don't include a human connection of any kind; they are not being paid for that.

I need to get out of the house. The walls feel like they are closing in on me...the large abode becomes increasingly smaller the longer I spend indoors. So, like most days, I head outside as soon as I'm finished eating. Stepping through the heavy double doors, across the threshold onto the large stone stairs, I feel the oppressive heaviness of the house lift off my shoulders. I squint at the sudden brightness and my eyes take a moment to adjust, but I welcome the light. The outside air is crisp and clean and I can finally take a deep breathe. I turn back only to look at the sizable iron door knocker in the shape of a crow holding a ring in it's mouth. It unsettles me, as though foreshadowing the enigmas within.

My feet know where they're taking me, and I start walking before I'm even really aware. Most every morning after breakfast, rain or shine, I head down to the water. Located directly behind the house, the grounds of the estate contain a small man-made pond leading into a swamp...or perhaps the swamp leads to the pond. I don't know.

I go for one reason and one reason only - to see the boy who lives in the pond. I approach the water's edge and scan the area, my hand shading my eyes from the brightness reflecting off the surface. It doesn't take me long to find him. He's standing in the water, up to his chest off to my right. I wave to him. He never acknowledges me, but he watches me. He never moves, but his eyes follow me as I walk up and down the shoreline. I know he'll never respond, but I talk away to him, telling him everything and anything, just to hear my own voice. I've no one to really talk to you see, so to me, he is my only friend. I call him Edward. From what I can tell, he looks to be around my age. There's nothing remarkable about him really, maybe his ears are a tad too prominent. Just a boy, with skinny shoulders sticking out of the water, and a small upturned nose. Oh, I know he's one of the shadow people, one of the ghosts...

I didn't know that at first. Not until the housekeeper, Mrs. Millicent Vandenhoff (I call her Miss Millie) came upon me at the pond one foggy day shortly after I had just come to live at Craymore Estate. Miss Millie is a proper British housekeeper if there ever was one. She's never seen out of uniform during the day, a simple black dress covered by a white apron. Her white hair is always up in a bun with soft tendrils curling down in front of each ear. She has a soft face, wrinkled with age and always serious. She's been employed by the family for about 40 years, Uncle Lewis once told me. She's been here though it all, the good times and bad, and has outlived many of the family members.

I was pacing back and forth, talking loudly to Edward, so my voice would carry over the water. I was gesturing wildly, animated in my story. I had attracted her attention when she looked out the window and came out to see what on earth I was doing.

"Why, I'm talking to that boy of course!" I pointed out into the middle of the water.

She looked out into the pond and then slowly back to me, her eyes wide.

"What boy?" She whispered with an intake of breath.

"He's right there. But why is he in the water? And why won't he tell me his name? He won't talk to me. Do you think he's getting cold?" I looked back at Edward, his wet brown hair plastered onto his head, his eyes staring back at Miss Millie and me. He stood stoically, not unlike the Queen's Royal Guards at the Palace gates, still and motionless, but ever vigilant.

"Child, there's no one there." Miss Millie raised her hand to her collar, pulling it together tightly, as if a shiver had just ran up her spine.

"Oh pish, he's looking right at you," I implored her to look, to see what I saw.

"Now that's enough. I don't want to hear such ghost stories. Get back in the house. It's damp and you'll catch your death of cold." She turned and headed towards the house, looking back over her shoulder to make sure I would follow.

I looked at Edward one more time, then back at Miss Millie. As I slowly followed behind her, the word "ghost" rolls over and over in my mind. It couldn't be...but why couldn't she see him? More importantly, why could I?

After Edward, I started seeing more of them. I hesitate to call them ghosts, actually. To me, ghosts are supposed to be transparent, floating beings who make scary wailing noises and try to frighten you. The beings I see often look as real to me as Miss Millie is. But then there are the ones I call the shadow people...they are just dark, mainly feature-less figures, exactly like shadows, which lurk in the corners. They were unsettling at first, but they've never tried to hurt me. They've never reached out to touch me, nor tried to scare me. So I have just accepted them. They live in the house too, simple as that. I've tried to tell the staff about them, tried pointing them out whenever I see one, but they've shushed me so many times, I've all but given up. I catch Miss Millie watching me out the window sometimes, as I talk to Edward, but she's never again come out to admonish me. Uncle tells me I'm scaring the staff and forbids me to mention it to them anymore. But I keep hoping that one day, something will happen, that he will be able to see...

iii:

Time passes very slowly in the old house. Every moment spent indoors feels like existing in another dimension, an eternity spent with the spectres, both alive and dead. I would try desperately to engage with the staff, make some sort of connection, feel accepted and wanted...but alas, they made it quite clear that they are workers only, not friends. Their sole obligation is to the house, not to me. I quickly got the feeling that I was underfoot and in the way. I would beg Uncle to take a break from his work and perhaps play cards with me, or go for a walk around the grounds. He always let me down gently, but always had an excuse why he couldn't be bothered. If he wasn't too busy, then he was too tired. Eventually I gave up trying to connect with the living and concentrated on the spirits around me.

Once I surrendered myself to the silence of the house and became aware of the unseen life it contained, it was like the house was alive in two dimensions. I would see Miss Millie go about her work dusting the furniture, and at the same time, I could see the translucent man sitting in the

Queen Anne chair beside her. I would be distracted
watching these two worlds occurring simultaneously
around me. The staff began giving me odd looks, as I
often appear to them to be a million miles away, focused
instead on watching the world of the spirits co-existing
with them. They see me silently staring off into space
more and more lately. In fact, I'm beginning to feel like
I'm not even here...like I'm one of them. The line between
living and dead is becoming blurred.

My head hurts more and more these days.

The old woman under my bed frightened me at first. The
first time she made herself known was when a withered,
old arm snaked it's way out from under the bed, reaching
up onto my mattress, feeling for my hand in the middle of
a moonless night. I was awoken by spindly fingers
grasping my own. From a solid sleep, my eyes snapped
open wide. Oh, but I was a brave girl. I hopped out of
bed, grabbed my dimly lit oil lantern and got down on the
floor. Kneeling down, I gingerly pulled up the blanket on
the bed revealing her aged, wrinkly features, her white
hair splayed beneath her. She lay flat on her back, lying

directly underneath where I lay my own head every night, staring straight up at the underside of the mattress. She turned her head and smiled at me, then faded away. I wasn't scared of her after that. She just existed...on some level, in some realm....

She just was.

My world felt larger than it had been in a long time. I no longer felt as lonely and insular as I used to. I stepped a little lighter in the halls as I did my daily walks around the expansive house, peeking out each gabled window, until I ended up in the attic - my favorite window of all – the circular window at the very top of the house. There I gaze out at Edward, forever standing in the pond.

The attic is by far my most favoured place to be. Although it is dark and dusty, it is also peaceful and quiet. No spirits linger here to distract me. My mind is clear and my brain can relax. The pain in my head even seems to subside. It is a calming place, where hours slip away from me, where I feel a little more like myself – and I haven't felt like myself is quite a long time.

Another reason I love coming up to the attic is all the items to explore. The room is full of furniture, boxes and trunks full of old world treasures from years gone by. There is something new to look at every time.

I enjoy, with anticipation, opening each box, each drawer to find the surprises within. Marvelling at the jewellery, baubles large and small, I try on every piece, modelling it in the impressive full-length mirror standing in the corner. Old ball gowns and tuxedos packed away are also modelled in my very own fashion shows, with the only audience being the odd mouse scurrying by. In the attic, I can just be the carefree child that I'm supposed to be, instead of the girl who has gone through tragedy after tragedy.

On this day, the attic welcomes me once again. I turn my oil lamp up as far as it will go and set forth opening a trunk located farther into the dark space. It's blue colour is scuffed and faded, and the lock is stiff and rusted. Leather strapping was meant to hold it all together, but it is frayed and rotted, falling away easily. With some effort, I'm able to raise the lid, wondering what I will find.

A musty smell rises from the long sealed box, causing me to crinkle my nose and I almost abandon this one, as it appears to be full of documents, papers and newspapers. But curiosity gets the better of me and I sit cross legged on the floor and begin to pull out piece after piece. Legal documents, ledgers, bank papers, deeds...none of this interests me. I dig down into the large trunk, leaning deeply inside, my feet almost coming off the ground, until my hands clutch upon something firm. Buried under all the loose paper and folders, I tug and yank, grunting with effort, until I pull out a large photo album. Wiping the sweat out of my eyes with the back of my hand, I sit back down on the dusty floor. The attic is indeed warmer than the rest of the house and the exertion of getting the album was discomforting. I pull at my jumper and loosen the button at my neck, before settling in to look at my find.

I carefully open the old book full of coal black pages containing vintage sepia, as well as black and white photos taped at the corners. Faces of the past gaze back at me, stoic and serious. Families sit as a group, expression-less.

Dapper looking men and stylishly dressed women, pose for photographers on settees or in front of the Estate's striking facade, which I recognize right away as it has not changed much outside from those early years.

I smile, looking at what must be relatives of some sort, and vow to bring the album to Uncle so he can name them all. This was my history, my legacy...my family. I am part of all this...a feeling of pride creeps in ever so slightly and I let it linger gently in the back of my mind. I do belong somewhere...I belong here, I'm rooted here. I set aside the album and dive back into the trunk.

At the very bottom of the loose leaf pages is a small wooden box, which I carefully lift out. There is a lock on it, useless, as it isn't latched tightly, so I'm able to open it easily.

What I find inside confuses me. It is a box of loose photographs – maybe only a dozen of them. More black and white pictures of men, women and even a couple children. Disturbingly, these pictures are burnt and blackened, making some of the pictures almost impossible to make out. It's as though they were in a fire and someone had grabbed them out and rescued them. Some are ruined completed, brittle burnt edges falling away when I touch them. Others are only partially destroyed. The pictures on the bottom are the most disturbing because not only are they burnt, but they are memento mori photographs. I have long understood that people in the olden days took pictures of their dead, as these were often the only pictures they would ever have of their loved ones, but I had never before seen any.

A chill runs up my spine as I gaze upon the pictures of people I know are deceased, their eyes either closed or glazed over. Loved ones sit beside them, or most morbidly, help prop the dead up to be photographed. The look of grief on the loved one's faces is painfully visible.

Studying the pictures make me feel a mix of heartbreak and empathy; bittersweet memories of mourning in my hands. People lost before their time, most of them young enough that they shouldn't have been near death's door. Slowly, with growing alarm, my skin begins to crawl. Terror gradually worms it's way into my heart as it skips a beat and a heaviness settles in the pit of my stomach. These faces look familiar... I've seen these faces before. A tightness grips my throat, breathing becomes difficult, and suddenly I can't get enough air. I fear I might faint. These are the faces that I see in the corners of my room, under my bed and in my closet. The final picture in the pile, charred around the edges like the others, is Edward standing on the grass in front of the pond in which he now rests.

In a flurry of panic and fear, my heart pounding wildly, I gather up the damaged pictures and race out of the attic, flying down the three flights of stairs bringing me to my Uncle's office door. It is closed and locked as usual. Jiggling the ornate gold handle mercilessly, banging and pounding on the thick wood, I call his name.

In moments, the door opens with a gust of wind rushing out at me and Uncle stands in front of me filling the doorway. His eyes squint with worry, his mouth agape.

"What on earth..." he begins.

Miss Millie comes rushing down the stairs, having heard the commotion. She's coming to admonish me I'm sure, but Uncle motions her away with a flick of his hand. She turns around and leaves, shaking her head.

"Uncle Lewis! What are these? Who are they?"

I thrust the pictures at him, into this chest, the force causing him to step back into the room. I follow him in. I've never been in Uncle's office before. It is a grand room, spacious with a mahogany desk sitting with it's back to large windows shrouded with long green velvet curtains. It is covered in file folders and papers, with a green banker's lamp resting on the corner. Wooden filing cabinets stand beside it, and along the opposite wall sits an impressive stone fireplace with a mantle full of framed documents and pictures, as well as vases of fresh flowers and nick knacks. I take only a brief moment to look around the room, remembering the reason for my interruption.

"Uncle, tell me!" I demand, sitting on a green fabric couch in front of the fireplace.

Looking at the photos, he sighs, leaning against the occasional table beside me. He rubs his eyes with one hand and then runs it through his hair. Tugging at his collar, he loosens his tie, cringing as if it's suddenly become way too tight. I look at him expectantly...waiting.

"You dug these out of the attic."

There's no emotion in his voice.

"Uncle Lewis," I begin, but my mouth hangs open, unable to continue.

How I want to tell him that I see them. I see these people! In this house! But how? How can it be? I plead with him to make sense of questions that have been swirling in my mind ever since the first time I saw the man in my closet...the one who wasn't really there.

"I wish you wouldn't be digging through things up there." His voice trails away as he flips through the photos, quickly, with barely a glance. It's obvious he's seen them before.

I don't reply.

Sighing he pulls out the photo of the old woman, dressed regally in a long dress and wide brimmed Victorian bonnet topped with flowers. I wish the picture was in colour, so I could properly envision everything about her. She isn't smiling, but she isn't frowning either, looking neither friendly nor unfriendly. She's looking directly at the camera, and if anything, she looks like she was bored or annoyed by the whole event; like posing for a photographer was something she had done a hundred times before and she was tired of the whole thing. As he is showing it to me, a million questions roll through my mind, but before I can say anything, he speaks.

"This is Mrs. Clara Craymore, nee Walker. She was my grandmother, mine and your father's of course - your great grandmother."

I don't tell him that she lies under my bed at night, peeking out at me, or holding my hand while I sleep. She's not trying to scare me, and since I've realized that, I find her presence actually comforting in some strange way. I view her as a nurturer, a mother figure of sorts. How bizarre that is, but I don't know how else to describe it.

Uncle Lewis continues, "Clara was a classy lady, always prim and proper, never a hair out of place. She was serious and solemn, but I also remember her as loving and caring. She didn't like to give hugs, but putting her hand on your shoulder was her way of letting you know she cared. She gave the best presents."

He chuckled a bit then, his eyes never leaving the picture as he reminisces, "I remember the year I turned 13. She gave me a buckshot rifle for my birthday. Can you imagine? My mother was fit to be tied, but she wouldn't say anything for fear of upsetting my father. His mother was financing her lifestyle after all."

I'm enthralled with his story, my eyes never leaving his face.

"What did she give my father on his birthday?" I want to

know, imagining my father as a little boy. I can't even
fathom what his childhood would have been like in this
house, surrounded by all this wealth. He had never talked
about his family or his upbringing. I had no idea what
background he came from until I saw Craymore Estate for
myself. I wonder why he wasn't proud to call it home, why
he ran from it all those years ago. But now is not the time
to bombard Uncle with extra questions. I don't interrupt
him as he continues to speak, gaining momentum with
every word, becoming lost in a past he has clearly not
revisited in a long while.

"Well, he was the lucky one. He was younger than me, as
you know. She favoured him, I believe, because he was
the baby. She presented him with a puppy, the year he
turned 6. He was thrilled, and all was well and good until
that puppy quickly turned into the largest dog we had ever
seen. She had gotten him a Great Dane you see." He
chuckles again.

These are tales I've never heard before and I cherish every
word. Hearing about my father, my family, is cathartic for
my wounded soul.

"Oh that dog would bound all over the house, until Mother found her voice and banished it outside, to hell with what her mother in law thought." He looked up at the ceiling with a small smirk on his face, remembering the past. "Many broken figurines and muddy paw prints all over floor up until then."

"What became of her?" I reach out and take the photo, looking into her eyes, wondering what colour they actually were – at night, under my bed, they just look like pools of black.

"Oh, she died shortly after this picture was taken. I don't think you need to know all the details."

He stands up, places the photographs on the table in front of me and walks to the window, looking out over the grounds.

"Yes, I do. I need to hear." I turn toward him, looking at the back of his pin striped suit, willing him to keep talking.

"Well, it's rather upsetting actually, because it occurred in your room."

A gasp escapes my lips and my heart starts beating so fiercely that I fear he will hear it.

"It used to be her room. You see, there was once a large armoire, that stood where your bed is now. It was made of hardwood, large and heavy. She was trying to reach something she had stored in a box on the very top of it. It fell over on her, crushing her instantly. She laid there for most of the day before she was found. That room, your room, was closed up for a long while afterwards, until the family decided to close and decommission the East wing. After that, it was opened and used again, as the East wing had held most of the spare bedrooms."

He turns back around, concern on his face, "Is this all disturbing for you to hear?"

"No. No. Tell me about the little boy." I urge him, pulling out the picture of the child I call Edward, the one in the pond.

He looks at it carefully.

"That's my cousin, Simon Craymore."

Simon. His name was Simon. Not Edward. Now that I know his proper name, maybe he'll respond to me.

"Simon was only 12 years old when he drown in the pond out back. As I remember being told, he had been trying to save a friend he was swimming with that was struggling under the water, but ended up drowning himself. His friend survived, but Simon was pulled from the water not breathing. He didn't live, he had taken in too much water. His lungs were full."

Uncle Lewis looks at the floor sadly. This is the most I've ever heard him speak since I've lived here. I am enraptured by his stories and his deep, gravelly voice.

Looking from him back to the photo, I run my fingers over Edward...I mean Simon's face. In life, he looked mischievous, fun, energetic...I'm sad that he never got to grow up.

I decide it's best not to let Uncle know that Simon never really left that pond. He rests there, in some form, to this day.

I touch my head tenderly as a dull ache settles in, but pull my hand quickly away before Uncle sees.

A couple more photos and I'm introduced to Philomena and James Craymore, my great uncle and aunt. They too, passed away in the house, five years apart, at the ripe old ages of 91 and 88 respectively. Nothing tragic there; lives well lived. I often see them in the sitting room, lounging in front of the fire, enjoying being in each other's company - white hair and wrinkled faces etched with laugh lines talking animatedly together in a language only they can hear.

Great great grandfather, Aloysius Craymore, the patriarch of the family passed away quietly in the gardens outside while tending to his prize roses. He was an avid gardener who spent many hours walking amongst his flowers. A big and imposing man with a thick and bushy handlebar moustache, he often traded his business suit in for denim overalls and rolled up sleeves to spend time in his beloved garden. It is believed that he had suffered from apoplexy and was found in death with a red rose clutched in his hand.

Aloysius had come to England as a child and became a well respected businessman, growing and honing his family fortune for many years. Now I know who the mysterious figure walking around the gardens is. He never acknowledges me on my morning walk-arounds; he's always focused on his plants and flowers, smelling each one over and one... in perpetuity it seems.

We come to the last photo, a man in a dress shirt and bowler hat, standing in front of a horse and buggy. The photo is blurry and grainy; it is difficult to make out his features. He appears to be tall and slim, but it is impossible to tell his age. I hold it out to Uncle, my head cocked quizzically.

He looks at it then looks away. If he thinks I didn't notice the pallor fall over his face, he would be mistaken.

"We've been talking forever, dear girl. I still have work to do..."

He's trying to dismiss me, but I'm not done learning and knowing all the mysteries yet. The home holds many souls, much history and loss and I need to know all of it.

Uncle Lewis sighs and sits down at his desk, picking up his pencil, flipping open his ledger book. When I don't leave the room, despite his obvious hint and fervent wish, he sighs, letting his pencil drop. It rolls off the desk and lands on the floor; he makes so effort to pick up it, but instead rubs his eyes with the heels of his palms. He tires of this conversation; spending so much time interacting with me exhausts him – but even more evident is the fact that there's something he doesn't want to talk about. I wait, until he fills the awkward silence with words.

"That would be my cousin, Henry Bennett Craymore. He was always a bit odd. He had a less than stellar personality, I'm afraid; rather morose and paranoid. He was always more sensitive than any of the other children, always easily offended, easily spooked."

Uncle Lewis looks up then, thinking out loud more than talking to me at this point.

"He was always skulking around the house, lurking, creeping. He'd appear out of nowhere and scare the bejeepers out of you just with his presence. He wasn't trying to, I don't think, it was just the way he was. As time went on, he became more and more sullen, increasingly disturbed, if you will. Something was affecting him and at first, he wouldn't say. He began to talk of seeing things..."

My ears perk up, "Things?"

"People, ghosts...I don't know. Everyone was worried about him, wanted him to get help, but he refused every offer to call the doctor in for a visit. The family spoke to the experts anyway, describing Henry's predilections, beliefs and behaviours. They were cautioned by each and every doctor that Henry was mentally unstable, likely diagnosable, but it was impossible to get a definitive diagnosis, what with his refusal to cooperate. They should have tried harder, because once he started to go down that slippery slope, it was only a matter of time before he..."

He looks at me then, cutting himself off abruptly.

"Are you sure you want to hear this? You are just a little girl after all. I don't want to be giving you nightmares."

"I am not a little girl!" My lower lip juts out petulantly.

Uncle begins to speak again, softer this time, as if to cushion the blow he knows is about to come.

"Henry insisted on changing rooms. He wanted, in no uncertain terms, to occupy my grandmother's room – Clara's room – your room. He moved himself in there and barely came out. At the end, he outright refused to leave the room. He died at only 19 years old."

Uncle Lewis stands up again and walks to the door opening it, encouraging me to leave, but I'm not having it and remain where I sit.

"Why did he want to stay in that room?" I need to hear the rest of this story – the rest of his young life.

Uncle closes the door, looking at the floor.

"He was adamant that he could see Clara in that room. He missed his grandmother and wanted to be close to her, to talk to her, he said. He told us that she 'lived' in there, even though she had been dead for many years by that point. The grown ups told us he was just trying to scare us kids, but it was obvious that they were worried about his mental state."

"How did he die?" I wait with bated breath for the words I know he's going to say.

"Oh love,...he hanged himself in the closet."

Even though I'm expecting it, the words are a crushing blow. Poor Henry remains in that closet, tied there literally and figuratively, gaping at me every time I open the door. He rests where he died, like the others, tied to this house. So much loss, so many lives.

I'm speechless, yet I have so many more questions. They rumble around in my head and try as I might, I can't put them into words.

"I suppose, now that you know, you'll want to switch rooms? I apologize for putting you in there, but when you first arrived, it was the closest and biggest room available for your needs, what with your wheelchair and all. Then you just settled in and I didn't have the heart to say anything or make you move. I was just hoping all this sordid history would never come up." He sits back down opposite me in a large velvet wing chair, resting his elbow on his knees and clasping his hands.

"No. No I don't think I need to change rooms, not right now anyway. But Uncle, there's something I don't understand." I look him in the eye, daring him not to tell me the truth, "Why were the pictures burnt? Who burned them?"

Uncle Lewis held my gaze.

"Why, Henry tried to burn them, even the picture of himself. He made a small fire in the bedroom in a bed pan using the long matches for lighting the oil lamps. He almost succeeded, and would have burned the house down, had the servants not been in the hallway cleaning, and smelled the smoke right away. They broke the door down, snatched the pictures out of the fire and put it out."

He pauses again, debating with himself whether or not he wants to tell me the rest. When he speaks again, he does so slowly and deliberately.

"Henry wailed that the pictures needed to burn because they haunted him, haunted his dreams, appeared to him every day and night. His thoughts and fears, his imagination, drove him crazy you see. It was that very night that he hanged himself with his belt. The poor maid found him the next day when she came to make the bed. He had sunk to his knees in the corner of the closet, his neck bent and eyes wide open and his mouth stretched into an exaggerated circle...."

My eyes are saucers themselves at this point. The images
of his stories are burned into my mind, along with the
images I'd seen for myself. Poor Henry, the experiences
he had drove him mad. I wonder why the spirits affected
him so. Although I'm grateful that they have not
terrorized, nor upset me, in the back of my mind I fear the
operative word is 'yet'. Each heartbeat spits out the
word...yet...yet... until the pain in my head becomes
unbearable and I thank Uncle for the information and take
my leave before he notices.

iv:

Days pass by, and I continue to think about all that Uncle
Lewis had told me. He has since reverted back to his
aloof and reclusive self, buried in his work, as though
opening his Pandora's box had deeply bothered him.
Maybe it's got him thinking also, remembering the past
and worrying about the future.

I thought knowing more would make me feel better, but
instead I find my senses heightened and my nerves frayed.

The headaches occur everyday, and I find myself tracing the long scar from my head down to my ear over and over again with my finger, in a self soothing manner. It doesn't relieve my pain, but it does let me know I survived...and I am not one of the others who walk the house, not understanding that they are dead. I'm alive...aren't I?

Things are getting cloudy, confusing...

Edward, I mean Simon, hasn't been in the pond for the past few days. I can't see him anymore. When I take my walks, the chill in the air is biting. Autumn is approaching, and with the changing seasons comes the feeling that something is indeed different. I can feel it in my bones.

One afternoon, I'm sitting on the stone steps of the entrance to house feeling sorry for myself, resting my hand on my chin and looking at the ground. My lot in life is not what I expected, nor deserve. I'm missing my parents a lot lately. Uncle is well meaning but I don't feel love for him. I don't know him, and he won't let me get to know him when it comes right down to it. He is a kindly benefactor, nothing more than a stranger really.

I like to think he has my best interests at heart, but lately I'm suspicious of everyone and everything. Perhaps he has brought me here to be a sacrifice to his house of horrors, which he presides over knowingly. I imagine him in his office making deals with the devil and laughing wickedly, but then I quickly shake my head as my worries and ideas being to run away with themselves. Of course, that's ridiculous...isn't it? Of course it is. Nonetheless, a feeling of impending doom simmers in my mind and I can't seem to shake it

As I'm lost in my thoughts, something catches my attention out of the corner of my eye. Turning my head I see a man walking up the long driveway towards the house. My curiosity is peaked immediately. His white dress shirt and tie, with red suspenders holding up his black pants, leads me to assume he has business with Uncle Lewis. Holding a cigarette between his thumb and forefinger, he takes a long drag, his eyes on the ground in front of him. He's moving slowly, with purpose, but does not look up at me. Craymore Estate does not get many visitors. My heart aches for human contact, so I'm thrilled to see someone new. I stand up and wave at him.

The man stops dead, about thirty feet in front of me in the large car courtyard. He finally notices me then, looking me in the eye. Under his thin, well-kept moustache, a sly smile began to spread. I begin to wave again, but quickly put my arm down. The smile has grown into a grotesque caricature on his face, lines deeply etched and extended wider than seemingly possible – his eyes are ebony black. A wave of dread washes over me and the urge to run becomes overwhelming, but I'm frozen to the spot, unable to look away. Goose bumps crawl over my skin; the hairs on my arms and back of my neck standing up like wispy spider-like legs. The air suddenly tastes like sulphur.

I wish I would have turned away or at least closed my eyes, but it happens too fast...in an instant, yet in slow motion. Before I can react, the man reaches into the back waistband of his pants and pulls out a pistol. Without any hesitation he puts it into his mouth and pulls the trigger. His cigarette falls to the ground, bouncing a couple times before it settles. He collapses in front of me, a splash of

red quickly turning into a crimson puddle beneath him –
and that's when I start screaming - shrieking and howling
loudly, until my throat is hoarse and my eyes are blinded
with tears.

Miss Millie is upon me quickly, but I'm hysterical. I can't
be calmed. I gasp and wail and sink to the ground. She
sits down there with me, shaking me by the shoulders.

"Child, child...what on earth is the matter? Are you hurt?"

She's trying to look me over, but I pull away.

The butler has joined her and he pulls me to my feet. My
eyes are shut tight, the image of what I had just seen
forever emblazoned in my mind.

Miss Millie sends the butler to get Uncle Lewis, and by
the time he arrives, my screaming has ebbed into
shuddering, hiccuping sobs.

"Leave us." Uncle sends the staff away and they scurry
inside, obviously shaken themselves

"What on earth are you screaming for?" he sounds annoyed. He doesn't know how to comfort a child, and is likely irritated at the intrusion in his day.

I point out into the driveway, refusing to open my eyes.

"What is it? Did you see a fox, maybe a snake? What is it, Adelia? For heaven's sake...," his voice trails away in exasperation.

I look then. The spot where the dead man had lay was bare – there was nothing there. I had imagined it...I must have.

"Uncle, there was a man...right there...he was walking...he shot himself. Right there, Uncle!" I urge him to look again. I'm truly confused and upset. The driveway is empty. I bury my face in his suit, the pocket watch in his front pocket hard against my cheek.

He pulls me away from him, hands on my shoulders and looks me in the eye. Taking his handkerchief out of his pocket, he dabs at my tear stained face.

"Come with me, we will talk."

He holds my hand and leads me back into the house. When the doors close behind me, I feel like I've been swallowed up into an abyss, into the mouth of Hell itself.

We sit in the Great Room, side by side on the satin chaise, a glowing fireplace crackling in front of us. The cherubs carved into the wood panels above the mantle stare at me accusingly. Taxidermied animals occupy the corners of the room, snarling and ready to pounce.

"I know you think you saw something..." he begins.

I immediately start to defend myself. I won't be patronized. I'm not crazy...am I? These days, I'm becoming less and less sure.

He put up his hands to shush me.

"Shh, just listen. I think I know what might be happening here. In fact, I've been wondering for some now, but have been loathe to say anything."

I look up at him expectantly, my eyes pleading with him to say something, anything to explain what is happening to me.

"Your father and I had a Great Aunt – that would be your great, great aunt. Her name was Twyla. She was eccentric, I guess that would be the best word to describe her." He ponders the memory for a moment, then exhales a short, scoffing breath through his nose before continuing, "She had unique ways of doing things. She dressed oddly – long colourful skirts, scarfs and baubles in her hair, gaudy jewellery adorned her neck and hands. It was just not how people dressed and acted, but it was her way. She even had a pet bird which she carried around on her shoulder, not unlike a pirate." He winked at me and I smiled slightly, not knowing where this was going, but not wanting to interrupt.

"She was my mother's aunt, and she lived here for a time, you see. The plans were for her to stay here permanently, as she had moved in after her husband passed away. But

Twyla only lasted several months before she fled. She claimed the house was driving her mad and she had to leave. I believe she left the country and moved in with one of her children in America, a place she had steadfastly refused to go initially.”

He clears his throat before continuing, “Twyla always claimed she had 'the sight'. She believed she could see and talk to spirits. She liked to read tarot cards and tell fortunes. A bunch of mumbo jumbo, we figured. My parents forbade her to do any of that nonsense when she was in our home. But, she began to be plagued with...visions...with...with...,” he stumbles over his words.

“She could see them...like me!” I exclaim, my heart leaping out of my chest.

Uncle hesitates momentarily before nodding.

“At first, the rest of the family didn't pay her any mind. She was always saying and doing strange things, so they ignored her claims at first. However, she began to get frightened by what she believed she saw. Her personality changed, she became fearful and teary, more often than not. She refused to leave her room, afraid of what she might encounter. She said she saw things that scared her, things she didn't understand. However, she was old enough to know the history of the house and the family members who had passed on before her. She knew she was seeing people who had once lived and died in the house. She never shared exactly what she witnessed...she didn't want to upset anyone else. Nevertheless, none of the rest of the family ever saw anything untoward.”

He stands up then, pacing around the room, the heels of his dress shoes clicking on the hardwood floors.

“I tell you all that, simply to tell you this...perhaps you have 'the sight'. Perhaps it's skipped some generations and landed with you,” he pauses, looking at me.

I am dumbstruck. Could there be an explanation for everything – could it be that simple?

“I've been listening to your claims of ghosts since you've been here. I must admit, it amused me at first, thinking my house was haunted. Then it unnerved me...scared my staff...I think once you realize that what you are seeing is not real, you can put an end to this. Oh sure, you might keep seeing things, but you can rest assured that they are not really there. It is in your mind. It is a gift inherited through the ages. So your job now is to control this gift before it takes over your life. We don't need another Twyla in the family." He ruffles my hair.

One thing still bothers me, one thing I can't get past.

"But Uncle, what about Henry? Did he have "the sight" too? He saw things. He saw things and he hung himself."

"Adelia, the consensus was that Henry was very mentally disturbed. His talk of ghosts was not real. It was his own mind driving him mad. The experts all agreed."

"Alright I'll try...I'll try to ignore it. I'll try to make it go away." I nod, not entirely convinced, but hope and faith are the only things I have to hold onto right now.

"That's what I like to hear. Now, do go and let the staff

know you are alright. They do worry, you know."

v:

Trying to see the 'gift of sight' as an actual gift was difficult. It seems more appropriate to call it a curse. Sometimes visions are obvious: people and scenes that play out in front of me; sometimes they appear as glimmers of movements caught in the edge of my vision, or shapeless, dark figures standing stoically in the corners of the room.

Most disturbingly, things are turning dark...unfriendly. Where I used to feel calm, I am now on edge. It started slowly, an imperceptible shift in their motivations, I suppose. If I look up, I may see something ethereal hovering above me, peering down at me; perhaps crouched under a table, a hand sneaking out to grab my ankle on the way by. These presences are no longer comforting; they are beginning to unnerve me. It seems they are trying to frighten me.

If I dare to tell Uncle, I'm certain he would only tell me

that I'm absorbing Twyla's story as my own, and that he never should have told me in the first place, then he would stop talking altogether. No, I must carry this burden alone for now. However, if I think too hard, I start to wonder if this is the truth. Maybe knowing what others experienced at Craymore is twisting my mind; my poor damaged brain unable to process it all.

I no longer feel safe wandering the halls of Craymore Estate. It seems something is out to get me..like they want me to join them. I don't know how to describe it, but ever since Uncle told me about Great Aunt Twyla, I can't help but feel that her fear and her need to flee were very valid.

I must even confess, that in my darkest moments during the night, as I lay awake listening to the grumbles of the house and it's inhabitants, I even start to wonder if I am Twyla....is that possible? Do I embody her – are we one in the same? I don't know what is true and what is not anymore. All I know is that my head aches something terrible.

Whatever dwells in the house is becoming violent, I dare

say. Although I hate to admit it. For instance, I was in the library the other day, which is located next door to Uncle Lewis's office. Oh, how I love to spend time in there, looking over the volumes of hardback books contained on the floor to ceiling shelves which surround the room. A fireplace and a large French window, rounded at the top complete the room. The oversized chenille couch is the perfect place to cozy up with a novel, which is precisely what I'm doing when Miss Millie comes in to dust.

She greets me with a curt, uncomfortable smile. She finds me to be an odd child, a troublesome burden for her employer. She looks upon me with an ever so subtle disdain and even suspicion. Although she never says anything untoward, I can see it in her face - the way she looks sideways at me, never directly into my eyes. Or how she will often go out of her way to avoid me if she can. She wishes I wasn't here. I wish the same.

I look back down at my book, trying to get lost in the words and she turns her back towards me, dusting the shelves nearest the fire place. At first, I'm not quite sure what happened. There was a rustle near my ear, as something whizzed past my head. A book, a heavy tome, seemingly shot out of the bookshelf, aimed at Miss Millie, indeed hitting her in the leg. Then another and another - unexpected and shocking.

She shrieks, dropping her duster, and whips around to stare at me angrily. She's certain I threw the books at her, but what else could she possibly think. They were missing from the shelf to my right, so the evidence is stacked against me. Besides, we are the only ones in the room...that she can see.

"Why did you do that? Why would you do such a thing?" She snarls, rubbing her leg.

"But, I...I didn't...honest Miss Millie, I didn't...." I stammer, standing up and walking towards her.

"Don't! Don't come near me! Stay away! There's something wrong with you, child!"

She wipes her face with the back of her hand, blinking back tears, picks up her duster and quickly limps out of the room.

I'm still bewildered, not understanding what just happened. I pick up the books, one at a time, and put them back on the shelf. The weight of those books in my hand feels...familiar...? No. I shake my head. I didn't throw them at her. It wasn't me! Was it? A chill runs up my spine, as though something cold had just brushed past me. Shivering, I look around the room. In the silence, I can hear something...

Wheezing...gurgling...

I climb back onto my big chair, on my knees, and look over the back. Crouched behind and looking up at me, was a dark figure – his only discernible features are eyes that seem to glow and a smile as evil as sin.

vi:

Miss Millie mustn't have mentioned anything to Uncle Lewis about the incident in the library, because nothing is ever said to me. She now avoids being in the same room alone with me, if she can at all help it. I avoid her as well.

I've taken to tip toeing around, peeking into rooms before

entering them, looking for creatures that shouldn't be

there. I don't understand why the spirits in the home are

becoming restless and angry. They never were before.

Although, it is safe to assume that if spirits exist, then

demons must also. That only makes sense.

I spend a lot of time in my room now, it seems the safest

place for me. My meals are left at my door on a tray,

which I eat alone in my room and place them back out in

the hall when I'm finished. I know the ghosts that dwell

here...Henry in the closet and Clara under my bed. Every

time I leave my room, I don't know who, or what, I'm

going to encounter. I don't know what to attribute the shift

to, but things are changing in this house. It's

disconcerting, and feels like it's building to a crescendo.

Uncle pleads with me to come out of my room, but I feel

safer locked in here. The dark figures seem to be attached

to me. They follow me around and I don't want to take the

chance that they might hurt Miss Millie again. I don't

want to get blamed for their actions, and no one would

believe me if I tried to explain. I won't tell Uncle what is happening. I don't want him to think I'm becoming like Henry or Twyla. If I think that I'm succeeding with a charade of normalcy, then I'm fooling myself. Nothing is normal right now, especially not me, but what other choice do I have?

The change in my behaviour concerns him. He worries about me becoming sullen and withdrawn, so he calls the doctor, an elderly man who has been caring for the Craymore family for many years, indeed outliving many of it's members. Dr. Gray, a kindly old man with white hair and a pocket watch hanging from a chain that he is constantly checking, pronounces me physically well, but we both know the struggle rages in my head. He tells Uncle not to worry too much, I just need more time to heal from the accident. Time heals all, he says on his way out the door, but I fear this statement is merely a foreshadowing. Time can heal...or it can be very, very cruel.

Nightmares begin to plague me; horrible and macabre images. Every night I dream terrible things, terrors that I remember vividly even hours later when light breaks. Visions of my room on fire all around me, as I lay in bed sleeping, unaware. I dream of Uncle being hurt, of Craymore Estate in flames, of being alone in the woods in the dead of winter. I force myself to stay awake long into the night, depriving myself and my brain of sleep, undoubtedly making everything worse. I refuse to succumb to sleep until it takes me without my consent, long after my lamp has burned dry of oil.

In the mornings, I look into the mirror and barely recognize the face I see there. She looks tired and weak, dishevelled and unkempt. And deep down I know that something is very, very wrong.

Uncle doesn't know what to do with me, he worries for my mental state and I know he's been making many calls, trying to get advice from experts. He threatens to send me away, have me committed. He begs for me to return to the land of the living, so to speak. He doesn't know how right he is, as I keep getting pulled into the world of the dead.

What occurred in the library with Miss Millie isn't the only odd happening causing me to question the shift in reality. Since I don't go outside much anymore, I keep an eye on the boy in the pond from my window. Simon has returned to his place in the pond, and each morning, I look out and ensure he's still there. His presence, always in the middle of the water comforts me, because at least that has stayed the same.

That is until one morning in mid September...

I wake up with the sun; it shines brightly into the room, dust particles dancing in the sunbeams. Squinting, my head is throbbing the moment I open my eyes, and I trace the scar from my head down to my ear over and over again, trying to calm and centre myself until the pain lessens to a dull roar.

Sitting up slowly, I gingerly place my bare feet on the cold floor. Standing up makes me dizzy, but the head pain does not get worse. As I do every morning, I head to the window to wave to Simon. I don't know if he can see me from this distance and probably wouldn't acknowledge me if he could, but he's the only one around here that is my age, so I feel a kinship to him. Isn't that strange?

When I pull the thick brown curtains aside and look out, I gasp. Simon is not in the water. He is standing on the shore, staring up at the house...staring directly at me in the window. The boy is clad only in his bathing trunks, looking out of place in the Autumn weather that had indeed left frost on the ground the night before. He stands still, not moving. his face blank. Seeing him out of the water is unnerving, and fills me with unease. My heart begins to flutter wildly, and despite the morning chill of the old house, a hot flush rushes over me, along with a sense of dread. Fearing I might faint. I grab the windowsill to steady myself. Closing my eyes, I look away, shaking my head... I must be seeing things...I must be imagining things. Nothing is as it seems. The throbbing in my head roars back to life.

When I look back outside Simon now stands several steps closer to the house, still staring up at my window. I jump back, alarmed. I don't understand what is happening.

I'm wedging a chair under the door handle when there are

several sharp knocks at my door. It can't be. It can't be Simon! I leap away from the door as if it's burning hot and run back to the window. Simon is back in the water, where he's supposed to be – not that that statement makes any sense in it's entirety. I breathe a sigh of relief. Maybe I imagined him moving. I'm really starting to worry that my mind is slipping.

"Adelia, open this door. I need to speak with you now." Uncle Lewis's voice sounds serious.

Reluctantly, I open the door and let him in. His brows are furrowed, a look of concern on his face. He rocks on his heels for a moment, unsure of himself, then sits on the chair at my vanity...Clara's vanity...my vanity.

"I don't like you being holed up in this room. I think it's time to stop this nonsense," he begins.

Before I have a chance to say a word, he tells me that he has hired me a tutor. He's grasping at straws and this is his answer to try and pull me out of myself and back into the world. A young man will be coming to the Estate twice a week to ensure I don't fall behind in my schooling. He

was loathe to put me in either private or public school

when I was sufficiently recovered from the accident. He

felt the added pressure of a new school was a stress I did

not need with such a head injury and ongoing recovery.

That was the last word said on the matter until now.

I begin to protest, but he holds up his hands and shakes

his head, saying this is non-negotiable. He feels that I'm

isolating myself. A tutor, he says, would give me some

much needed socialization, draw me out of the shell I am

creating around myself. He goes on to lecture that

education is important and I have a lot to catch up on after

the accident. I suspect he also wants someone to keep an

eye on me, report back any strange behaviour or

happenings to him – to be another set of eyes and ears. I

don't want a babysitter, but there is no changing his mind.

Done is done, and it is set in stone.

 As he is leaving my room, the large wooden framed

picture of Thomas Gainsborough's Blue Boy which hangs

on the wall opposite my door, falls crashing to the floor,

splitting the old frame into splinters. It takes Uncle by

surprise, but his shock quickly turns into dismay. He
loves that picture, the little boy posing for the artist is one
of his prized possessions, even though he has many more
impressive paintings. It has hung in that spot for many
years. I, on the other hand, grew to abhor that picture, ever
since I first saw it. Initially, it reminded me of Simon, but
as time passed, that is exactly the reason I no longer like it.

Uncle believes the picture falling was an accident. He
couldn't see the hand that had pulled it off the wall. After
he cleans up the pieces and heads back downstairs with the
mess, I close and lock my door....leaving the figure
standing where the picture had been, smirking
maliciously.

vii:

The tutor's first visit is to be two days from now. Uncle
had insisted that lessons be held at the dining table, but I
put my foot down and in no uncertain terms let him know
that I would not be leaving my room. Uncle relented, only
because I pitched such a fit.

Mr. Smith-Bellows is only 25 years old, if he is a day. He is younger than I thought he would be, a welcome sight, as I was expecting a grouchy old codger who would bore me to tears or smother me with strictness. He's dressed sharply in a suit jacket and tie, his dark hair slicked back off his chiselled face. He has a rather regal look about him, perfect posture and clean shaven face.

When he introduced himself, he told me with a kindly smile, to call him by his given name, Jonathan. He comes dutifully twice a week on Tuesdays and Thursdays and we sit at the desk in my room discussing maths and sciences and literature. Perhaps it is a young girl's crush on an older man, or perhaps it is the lure of a stranger, but something unexpected begins to happen - I quickly begin to look forward to his visits. I wait at my window at 9 am twice a week until I see him pull into the courtyard and head towards the house. I find myself enjoying debating the meaning of the writings of Kafka and Dostoevsky. Even trying to make sense of numbers becomes not an arduous task, but a verbal sparring in which I learn unintentionally. I appreciate the stimulation and the company, more than I care to admit. He's a breath of fresh air...illuminating, like a thunderstorm at midnight. He challenges my mind, listens to my opinions, and treats me...like I exist...for too long I have felt invisible in this home.

In addition to all these things, the most important result of Jonathan's presence is that the ghosts and hauntings don't happen when he is here. At first I was terrified that they would show themselves and scare him away, but they keep silent. The feeling of peace he brings with him is a huge relief; a period of calm. However, after he leaves, they awaken stronger than ever, becoming evermore malevolent. Are they jealous that something is taking my attention away or do they want something of me? Their activity increases alarmingly, and they are most definitely trying to scare me. My window will fly open in the middle of night, even though I know I locked it. When I get up to close it, it slams shut, narrowly missing my fingers. My oil lamp will blow out as I am reading in bed at night. My books and trinkets randomly fly off my shelves. And the nightmares become all the more disturbing...at least I hope they're nightmares. They are all too real, and if I'm being honest with myself, I don't know whether I'm awake or asleep... I confide in no one and I stay in my room. I feel like this is my battle to wage, and my burden to carry.

The old woman under my bed has remained quiet...until now. She begins speaking to me in hushed tones, words that I can barely hear. She is no longer a comforting presence; she frightens me – her face is no longer grandmotherly and pleasant, it has become hardened and etched with fury. Her gnarled hand snakes onto the bed during the night and grabs at my hair, pulling my head down over the edge so she can snarl into my ear. She tells me evil things, trying to convince me to do her bidding...wanting me to break things, burn things, hurt others. I battle with her, I battle with my own mind...and through it all the headaches rage on and on.

The impending Winter has brought with it a chill in the air that has settled around the Estate. In the mornings, a blanket of ethereal fog hovers above the pond, as the weather shifts seasons. Sometimes I can barely see Simon until almost noon, when the fog finally burns away in the sun. My room is warm and cozy like a welcoming blanket, so it is odd that I have chosen now, of all times, to venture outside for the first time in weeks.

I had a dream last night...it seemed so real...I dreamt of my parents. They were smiling and happy, dancing in the middle of the road, with the upturned car beside them in the ditch. Blood ran down their faces, bruised and battered from the accident. Their clothes were torn and their skin pale as death, yet they were beaming, waltzing in the road to music only they could hear. Even though it was a gruesome scene, I awoke with a smile on my face and a realization in my heart. Anyone who dies on the grounds seems to be tethered to the spot of their demise...Clara where the armoire lay, now where my bed is... Henry in the closet... Aloysius in the gardens... Simon in the pond. My parents, they died on the grounds, on the long winding road to the Estate, but on the grounds nonetheless. I need to know...

I bundle up in my heavy woollen coat lined and trimmed with fur, pulling the belt tight around my waist. The otherworldly rumblings begin as I open the door – it's apparent the spirits are not pleased with my movement. I lock them away in the room and venture out.

The butler smiles and tips his hat politely when he sees me in the halls, and even Miss Millie gives a polite smile and nod as I walk down the grand staircase and out the front door. But was her smile just that? Or maybe she was hoping I would wander away and never come back. I shake that thought from my head. Intrusive notions have started to plague me, causing me to question and second guess everyone and everything. Even Uncle Lewis's intentions cause me to lay awake and ruminate at night. I'm not sure where the paranoia is coming from, but it leads me to wonder why he agreed to take in a child, a virtual stranger to him. Did he actually know what he was bringing me into after all? That the house would affect me so? Does he even care that it's causing me to feel like I'm losing my mind?

Outside, I walk past Simon, past the man in the gardens, perpetually smelling his flowers, now frost bitten and dying. I don't look at either of them. I walk around the front of the house and start down the long driveway. Tall trees line either side, standing straight in line like a row of soldiers.

Along the open road, the wind blows cold, the first serenade of winter's song. The air is filled with an ominous brittle silence, save for the shrill trilling of the occasional waxwing announcing it's seasonal arrival. The sound pierces my head painfully. I walk lightly, slowly but with purpose, my shoes crunching on the leaves and gravel under my feet.

I will never forget the exact spot of the accident. It occurred on the only straight stretch of the winding laneway. I round the final curve and it lays before me. Time has passed and changed the landscape some, but the crushed, charred brush on the side of the road marks the spot. I can still picture the car upside down, as my eyes opened briefly when they pulled me out. The brief flashback causes a zap to flit through my head and I take just a moment to rub my temple and steady myself before stepping off the road and sitting on a rock next to the accident scene. It is the rock which went through the windshield, connecting with my father's face as the car landed on its roof. I'm lost in memories and sadness, remembering a life that once was, and love that is now gone.

It begins as a rustle, a whisper in the breeze. I think I hear my name.

I look up, cocking my head, listening.

"Adelia...."

It is clearer now, a long, drawn out breathy voice.

"Mother?" I stand up, looking around. The air has changed, it is completely still now, and there is absolute silence, as though I'm suddenly in a void, in a different world.

She appears in the trees, transparent and graceful, holding her hand out towards me.

"Come to me..,"

I hear it in my head, not my ears.

She fades away....she fades in and out...

"Come with me..."

My head hurts and I close my eyes. When I open them she is gone. The birds begin to chirp again.

The spell, whatever it was, has been broken. I'm disappointed, but hopeful and I know I will visit again. My parents can indeed be found here, and with them, a calm and peace that my heart has been yearning for. The sun is starting to fall beneath the trees, and I know I must head back, lest I be missed. I won't be telling Uncle Lewis, he wouldn't understand.

I am in such good spirits when I return to the house, that I feel up to sitting at the big dining table and having dinner with Uncle. Only a handful of times has he ever eaten with me. He is so happy to see me out of my room and participating in real life, that he makes a point of be here with me tonight. The mood is light and we have a jovial conversation. He asks me how my tutoring sessions are going, and I admit I'm enjoying them. He seems so pleased by the end of the meal that he leaves the room with a smile on his face, ready to hole himself up in his office again, convinced that everything is right in his world.

I fall into bed that night with a sense of renewed hope and joy. Having the opportunity to reconnect with my parents has made all the difference and lifts a weight from my shoulders that I never knew was so heavy. For once, there are no bad dreams.

For the next few nights, the ghosts are quiet...but their placidity is deceptive.

viii:

A bitter wind whistles through the cracks of the house, flapping the shutters loudly, jarring me from a deep sleep. The oil lamp sitting on the windowsill burns dimly, with the flame flickering and dancing with the breeze. The old house is drafty, and moans and groans in the inclement weather.

The floor is cold on my feet as I get out of bed and go to the window. The flame of the oil lamp reflects on the glass and the only thing I can see when I look out the window is my own face, both eerily lit and shadowed, as well as the nearby branches scratching persistently in front of me. The night is pitch black,with no moon to be seen.

Sighing, hoping I can get back to sleep, I turn back towards my bed on the opposite wall. My foot hovers in mid air, refusing to take the first step, when I hear a long, slow creak. Hesitantly, I look to my right. I know what that sound is. The closet door has open several inches and it is still moving. I stumble backwards, backing away as far as I can go until I hit the writing desk in the corner with my hip. The pain doesn't even register; all my attention is focused in front me. As the door finishes opening all the way, the dull oil lamp suddenly flares brightly, illuminating the room with a shadowy glow.

Henry, normally hunkered down in the corner of the closet, forever attached to the noose he hung himself with, is standing upright on his feet. As I watch in horror, he un-hangs himself – taking the noose from around his neck and dropping it on the floor. When the noose hits the ground, so does he. Falling to his knees, he emerges from the closet, crawling out on his hands and knees, his bent neck lolling to one side unnaturally. He's looking at me sideways, as he creeps and slinks towards me. A low guttural growl emits from his throat, as he gasps for air with an impossibly twisted airway.

I'm frozen to my spot, having wedged myself deep into the corner beneath the desk. He's mere inches away from me and he's reaching towards me...

And then I scream.

Slamming my eyes shut, shrieking like a banshee, I'm hysterical and inconsolable. Uncle runs into the room. Miss Millie follows in her dressing gown, carrying a brightly lit oil lamp.

Uncle pulls me out from under the desk, and my screams have ebbed into shuddering sobs. My eyes are scrunched closed so tightly it hurts and tears run down my face.

"What's wrong? Oh my lord, what's wrong child?" His voice is fraught with alarm and fear.

Miss Millie clutches the top of her ankle length dressing gown together at the neck, her eyes wide.

I wipe my eyes, opening them tentatively.

I tell Uncle that nothing is wrong, even as I watch Henry crouching behind him and Miss Millie. He is squatting on his haunches, long fingernails scraping against the wooden floor, as though he's getting ready to attack.

Uncle is asking me if I'm alright, if I've had a bad dream. He's shaking me lightly by the shoulders, trying to get me to speak, but my eyes are glued to Henry as he crawls back into the closet, eyes full of fury.

"Yes, Uncle Lewis, a very bad dream." I whisper.

My head is throbbing and I pass out, falling into his arms.

ix:

I wake up to find Dr Gray standing over me, as I lay in my bed, covers pulled up to my chin.

He pats my head and says something in a comforting, grandfatherly way, but I don't hear him over the pressure and murmurings in my head. He then joins Uncle Lewis at the door, talking quietly.

The sun is beginning to rise, the darkness in the room being washed away by the light, telling me that a few hours have passed. Shadows on the wall become smaller and the fears of the night before are quickly becoming forgotten.

Uncle Lewis pats the doctor on the back, thanking him for coming at the ungodly hour that he did, and lets Miss Millie escort him out.

The outline where the Blue Boy painting was hanging across from my room is exceptionally obvious – a bright white square in the middle of an otherwise faded wall. I must ask Uncle not to hang it there again once it's repaired. I can't bear to look it, I fear one day it will start talking to me.

He closes the door and returns to my bedside. I smile and assure him I am fine and apologize for waking him and causing so much trouble.

He looks tired, concerned; his brow furrowed, his face serious. He tells me he will cancel my lessons for this week, but I sit up and protest. I tell him I'm fine and I want to see Jonathan. If he cancels, I will refuse to eat. I will hold my breath. I will throw myself out the window...

He doesn't know what else to say or do. He pats my hand and relents, leaving the room. I sleep soundly, a deep and dreamless sleep.

Jonathan Smith-Bellows has a laugh that affirms his name, a deep, hearty chortle of mirth that one can't help joining in. I love listening to it, as he makes a joke he thinks is terribly funny, and can't contain his merriment. I perch my chin on my hand, elbow on the table, enraptured with his discussion of Shakespeare, as we eat cheese and fruit prepared by Miss Millie.

"Of course, my favorite quote is from Troilus and Cressida: 'He hath not so much a brain, as ear-wax'. This play is both a tragedy and a comedy, you see." He sputters, one hand on his belly as he chuckles.

I smile, "Shall I offer my own favorite quote professor?"

"Please do," he encourages, wiping a tear of laughter from the corner of his eye.

"'Hell is empty and the devils are all here.' The Tempest, Scene 1, Act 1."

He stops laughing then, straightening his vest beneath his suit jacket uncomfortably. There's a brief awkward silence. He picks up the kitchen knife and slices himself a piece of firm cheese, putting it down again before he speaks.

"Well, yes...that's a good one too, of course. Great play, The Tempest. How do you know the works of William Shakespeare so well, dear girl?"

"The library downstairs, of course. It's full of all sorts of books." I nod demurely.

This was only partly true, but he didn't have to know that Clara whispers many such things in my ear during the night.

Jonathan must never know. What would he think of me?

He excuses himself and goes downstairs to pour himself another cup of tea, as Miss Millie has not brought up the tea pot up for him.

I sit and wait patiently, closing my eyes to rest just a spell, as all this thinking today has taxed my sore brain. In the silence, I hear a whisper, barely perceptible words. I turn and look behind me. Clara's hand is out from under the bed, motioning me urgently to come to her. I look to the door, worried that Jonathan will walk in at any moment, but the hallway is quiet. I go to her then, kneeling down by the bed. As soon as I'm close, the hand grabs my collar roughly and pulls my face close to the floor.

What she tells me then is upsetting. What she wants me to do is unmentionable. Yet, she is compelling, persuasive and my mind isn't all that stable right now, you see.

When Jonathan comes back into the bedroom carrying the teapot, I am waiting for him behind the the door with the long, serrated cheese knife in my hand. Why am I doing this? Why does she beckon me to do her bidding? I'm not in control right now, even though I know precisely what I am doing. I'm fighting with myself, reasoning with myself. I don't want to do this. The internal struggle causes me to tremble, sweat beading on my brow. I won't do this! I won't, Clara!

He sets the teapot on the table gently, then looks up, noticing I'm gone. He turns around and sees me partially hidden by the open door. He looks quizzical, then disturbed, then horrified. His face contorting through the various emotions.

The knife is clenched in my hand so tightly that my knuckles are turning white and locking in place. He doesn't know how hard I am fighting right now. My right foot moves forward, then my left and I charge. He backs away in alarm. I manage not to raise the knife, fighting with Clara for control over my own limbs. I only take a few steps, then my eyes roll back in my head and I collapse to the floor, a seizure overtaking my body. While I flail and twitch on the ground, the knife falls out of my hand, and the last thing I see is Jonathan bent over me, alarm on his face. But he's alive. He's still alive. I win, Clara.

x:

Uncle had insisted I go to the hospital, where I spent a few days having tests, all of which came back normal, and letting my poor brain heal. The pain and fatigue were unbearable at first. But I got better quickly, so quickly in fact, that they could not find a reason to keep me. Against Uncle Lewis' better judgment, they sent me home, where I continue to recuperate in bed for another couple days. But even now, days later, I feel like I have been hit by a truck.

Jonathan hadn't realized what peril he was in. If he had have, I'm sure I would have been in a very different kind of hospital. I thank the heavens for small favours.

Lessons are cancelled for the foreseeable future. I am disappointed that I won't be seeing him, but only I understand it is for his own safety, so I don't protest. He best stay away from me; there's something wrong with me. The ghosts are becoming...troublesome, malicious....murderous. I don't know why, but I must protect those around me.

During the day I lay in bed, watching the clock tick away the hours, being waited on hand and foot. I spend most of my time worrying and wondering how to rid of myself of the evil that has attached itself to me. At night, in the dark, I talk quietly to Clara, to Henry, pleading and reasoning with them to behave, to leave me alone, to spare my family. They don't reply. They have been silent since the incident with Jonathan. I talk to God, the heavens, the universe, a silent prayer to whatever could possibly help me. I feel all alone in the world.

Eventually boredom overtakes me and I insist on being let out of bed. I have been yearning to go back and try to visit with my parents again. Maybe they can give me some words of wisdom, perhaps help in some way. I don't know what else to do. Even though I know they are dead, I need their comfort.

Uncle Lewis agrees it will be good for me to resume my walks around the grounds. He says the fresh air will do me a world of good. At first, he insists that someone accompany me, just in case. So, the butler walks with me a few mornings, elbow gently linked with mine, as we meander around the Estate. We don't talk much; he is only doing his duty – and I am merely appeasing Uncle Lewis until he believes that I'm indeed alright. We pass Simon standing in the pond and I can't help but stare. His hands are straight at his side and he does not move, but his eyes watch intently and follow me from one side of the pond to the other. The butler looks at me and then out into the pond to see what has has captured my attention so completely. Of course, he does not see it. He just shakes his head and leads me forward.

As soon as I'm able to go for walks on my own, without being hovered over, I immediately head to the accident site. There is now a light blanket of snow covering the ground, but this day is mild. Tightening the scarf around my neck that Uncle Lewis insisted I wear, I slip on my warm hat and gloves. Always a practical man, Uncle thinks that his diligence means everything is status quo. As long as he does what is right, then everything is fine. In his world, money can fix everything and making more money is the obsession that keeps him going. It is what he focuses on to hide from everything else. Such a simple, clueless man.

My father was a more complex man. I don't know that he was ever so sure of himself. Unlike his brother, he never took life in stride because he knew that the world wasn't going to fall into place just because he did what he was supposed to do. No, my father knew life was more complicated. There were things that ate him up inside and I believe now that his past had affected him, leaving him serious and stone faced most of the time. What he had experienced in this house as a boy had to have traumatized him, I understand that now. He ran from his childhood and his past in order to create a new future, but in the end, no matter how far he ran, his past dragged him back and defeated him. But at least he experienced a life away from here – this all consuming, godforsaken place.

It is early in the morning, as I woke with sun and headed out before I would be missed, in order to give myself more time with my parents. There is so much I want to say to them, so many questions I need answers to. Why did they leave me here alone? Why did we suddenly need to go to Craymore – what matter was so pressing that is hastened their deaths? Why am I left to suffer the wrath of the unsettled ones in the house? Most importantly though, I need to feel their love and the reassurance that we will be together again. Contemplating my fate and fearing the unknown, I walk on, leaving the house to fade away behind me.

The tall trees, ever green, line the winding path I'm coming to know so well. Around the last corner, comes the clearing where my life changed forever, and where I last saw my mother...in both corporeal and non-corporeal form. Sitting on the same rock as last time, I pull my coat tightly around myself and wait. How I wish I could turn back time, that none of this had ever happened. What I wouldn't give to be family again, in our old home, far away from this strange place.

Thanks to the accident, I don't remember a lot of things that happened before we set out on our journey to the town of Ashby, father's childhood home. My long term memory was impaired terribly. Doctors promised it would recover to some degree, but it is patchy, and memories of my past life are murky and hazy at best. But I remember being loved.

Time passes without even so much a hint of their presence. I start to wonder if I had imagined seeing my mother the last time I was here, but I could hear her voice as plain as day. I could be wrong...I could be crazy. Maybe my mind has been playing tricks on me after all. I don't know what is true anymore. I shake my head, trying to rattle out the cobwebs, trying to shake it clear and make sense out of the world. It always feels like my brain is in a fog; thinking hurts, trying to remember hurts...and not knowing what is real hurts most of all.

The longer I wait in the silence, the more impatient I become. I can't be gone too long or Uncle will come looking for me, and I can't be found here. A few flakes start to fall, breaking loose from the fluffy, swollen clouds as I look around waiting for my parents to show themselves, willing them into existence. I can't give up hope. If I do, it will mean that my parents are dead and gone with a finality I cannot cope with. My eyes are blurry and my head is aching something terribly, but hope is all I have, so I wait.

Finally, my patience is rewarded when they appear across the road. They are standing in between two towering trees, holding hands. I stand up and take a couple steps, a beaming smile on my face...until I notice, in shock, that they look like they've just come out of the wrecked car, like the accident had just happened.

My mother is no longer pristine and beautiful. Her simple navy blue belted dress is torn, one sleeve wide open at the shoulder. Her long auburn hair, perfectly curled, is matted with blood. One eye is swollen shut, the other slightly bulging. Her leg is bent at an impossible angle, but she is smiling as she stands beside my father. He, himself, looks just as awful. One ear has been ripped off, and his jaw is hanging off on one side revealing his teeth and gums. His left foot is twisted, facing completely backwards, pointing into the woods behind him. He tries to smile, yet his face is hardly recognizable; dripping with blood, crushed from the impact of the rock through his windshield.

I back away in horror, as they began to walk across the road towards me. They aren't looking at me however, as they veer off to the left and continue on down the road. I watch them walk off into the distance and get into the black sedan that is parked on the shoulder. It's our old car, in perfect condition, nary a scratch, sitting with its engine idling. They let go of each other's hands and part ways at the front of the car, getting in on either side. My father is at the wheel as they pull onto the road and begin to drive towards me.

The car quickly accelerates and they are speeding as they

approach me. I jump back into the ditch to avoid being hit. Without warning, the car breaks suddenly, sliding through the gravel, then lurches forward again. I can see the look of terror on my mother's face through the window, her hands in front of her, trying to ward off the impending blow. Even more terrifying, as the car passes by, I see myself in the backseat. My hands are pressed up against the back window, my face contorted in fear, mouth open in a scream.

As I watch horrified, the car hits the shoulder and flips over and over, landing on its roof on the rock in front of me with a sickening crunch. Then complete silence.

I've just witnessed the accident, as it had happened, all those months ago. But how? My hand flies to my mouth to stifle a scream and for a moment, I'm glued to the spot until I find my legs. They shake uncontrollably as I walk tentatively towards the car, upturned wheels spinning. Smoke pouring out the underside quickly turns into flame and within seconds, an explosion rocks the car. I cannot hear anything over the crackling fire and the pressure in my ears. The air fills with acrid black smoke and the smell of gasoline, burning my nose. Coughing uncontrollably, I kneel to the ground, choking and crying. When I look back up again, the car is gone, as is the carnage around me. Stumbling backwards in a daze, I hear a noise....a car idling....

Looking back down the lonesome road, I see my parents once again get into the car. It's happening again - the scene plays out once more. The car comes speeding towards me, lurching in the road, hitting the shoulder and rolling over and over – coming to a crunching stop on the rock near me.

I don't understand what's happening. Sinking to my knees, I sob uncontrollably until my lungs ache. As my eyes are closed, I hear the scene play out a third time...and then again. Over and over the car crashes next to me...then..silence.

Hesitantly, I open my eyes. Everything is clear. There is no car crash, no fire... Blinking tears away, I stand up and look around. It is over.

My mother stands in front of me, uninjured, smiling. She holds her hand out towards me, motioning for me to follow her.

"Come with me."

Her lips don't move, but I hear her voice.

She turns her back to me and begins walking away, revealing the back of her head - it is a mess of bone and tissue, crushed and bloody. When she turns back to smile at me her face is dripping with blood.

I run away from her, towards the Estate and I don't look back.

xi:

I return to the Estate and take to my bed, staying there for days, despondent and depressed. The reunion with my parents was not what I expected and I'm devastated. Seeing the crash over and over again from an outside perspective...seeing myself in the backseat...it was all just too much. I shut completely down, refusing to eat or speak for several days. I just lay there night and day, staring at the ceiling.

Uncle Lewis, in his concern, intends to tell the doctor I'm catatonic and need to be hospitalized at once. He's certain I have some sort of illness of the mind and need to be diagnosed in a special hospital. He sits at my beside and tells me of his intentions, thinking I'm so far gone that it doesn't matter. But it does matter and I need answers. When he gets up to call the doctor, I begin to scream; maniacal, bloodcurdling screams... first sounds uttered in several days. Savage inhuman sounds, not of this world...

Startled, he whips back around to look at me and rushes back to my beside.

With tears in his eyes, he gets on his knees beside the bed and whispers, "Child, tell me what's wrong."

I stop screaming and slowly turn my head towards him. My face is distorted – my lips curled into a peculiar, exaggerated smile; my eyes empty and wide, glare back at him, unblinking. He backs away from the bed, hand on his chest in fright.

For only a moment, I feel like I've completely lost my mind – that it no longer belongs to me, that someone else is in there. But that moment is fleeting and I'm quickly back to my old self. Breaking down into tears, I sit up and begin to sob. He comes back and holds me until I make his suit coat wet with tears. He shushes me and calms me, until I regain my composure.

“Uncle...” I hiccup, trying to breath, “What is happening?”

He's at a loss for words, so he just hugs me tighter.

“Don't call the doctor, Uncle Lewis. I'll all be alright, honest I will. Promise me, Uncle.” I looked up at him, pleading, “I'm feeling much better now. I think I'm hungry, in fact.”

I pull away and smile at him. I need to buy myself some time to figure things out, to try and put a stop to the madness I find myself in.

Uncle Lewis desperately wants and needs for me to be normal, whatever the loose definition of that word is right now. So, he believes me, in order to maintain the illusion that everything remains the same in his world. He refuses to open his eyes and see what is in front of his face. How easy it is to be raving mad around him; he chooses to look the other way. Perhaps it is not his fault, having lived with madness since he was a child. It may well be woven into the threads of this family, embedded so deeply, he no longer recognizes it. For all I know, maybe he struggles to hold onto his own sanity just the same...

Uncle assures me he won't call the doctor, not this time anyway. But he promises he will if this ever happens again. I nod in agreement, to assuage him...anything to make the threat of hospitalization go away.

In my research in the library downstairs, I've read about what happens to people who are hospitalized with diseases of the mind - how their brains are electrocuted with shock and scrambled with ice pick lobotomies, how they are put on such harsh drugs that they are never themselves again. They become drooling shells of themselves - experimented on, neglected, left to rot in solitary rooms. No, that won't be me. I will never let that happen. I don't care what I have to do, I will prevent that scenario. I'd rather die than end up in that state at the mercy of some heartless hospital staff.

So for the next days, it takes all my might and energy to act as normal as I possibly can. I'm barely keeping it together. During the day, I resume my walks around the Estate, pretending I don't see Simon or Aloysius. I try to ignore the rumblings of Clara and Henry, even though they are getting louder and louder.

During the night, the closet door creaks open and Henry, forever crouched in the corner under my Sunday best dresses with his neck permanently bent to one side, stares at me, unblinking. Sometimes a low growl emits from his throat. I don't know why. I don't know what he wants from me. Sometimes I think he wants me to join him,

Clara...well Clara is more forthcoming with her intentions.

When the clock strikes one in the morning and the rest of the house is in a sound sleep, Clara spouts rage-filled threats, trying to cajole me into doing her bidding. She wants everyone to die...she wants to use me as her vessel to do so. She wants to climb right inside me and take over my mind...make me do evil, unspeakable things. And I must fight with her every single moment to ensure this doesn't happen. Her will is strong, but I must be stronger. From what I've been told, in life, she was a wonderful, matronly woman. But in death, she's been turned into an awful, homicidal creature. It's not really her, you see, it's this house.

I've come to the conclusion that it is the house itself, that tethers it's inhabitants here, that causes the shift in their personality, the change in their mental state, beginning in life...with the transformation being complete after death. The house must be evil. I don't know why, but after many hours of mulling things over in my head, in a dark quiet introspection, I know this for certain... as sure as I know that the house intends to take me too one day.

This has to be true. This has to be the answer to the

mystery, because the alternative is even more horrifying...too horrifying to entertain – because the only other thing that can be true is that none of this is real. The only other explanation is that I am insane. Maybe my brain never did heal... the headaches do occur almost daily, a subtle, dull throb deep inside the very centre of my head.

Or could it be, that I am actually in a coma, in some hospital, and my body is raging a war to live, which is being played out in my mind? Maybe I'm already dead...and this is my own private hell. Either way, there's something very wrong with me.

The Craymore Estate is a living, breathing being, inside and out. The walls have ears, listening to the faintest whispers, knowing my thoughts and reading my mind. The ghostly inhabitants watch my every move. It's difficult not to feel paranoid and suspicious of everyone, living or dead.

I know Uncle Lewis has Miss Millie and the butler keeping an eye on me for him. I catch them watching me, while they pretend to do something else. If I'm outside, I can look over to the house and see one of them peeking out at me behind the curtains. They are trying to catch me doing something or acting in some way that they can report back to Uncle Lewis to have him send me away. I become convinced that they want to see me lose my mind and put in a hospital. They never did really like me. They can't wait to get rid of the burden they've been entrusted with caring for, even though the imposition only extends to basic necessities, as they provide nothing more. They figure it's only a matter of time.

So I try with every ounce of strength I possess to be normal, even though my mind is betraying me. If a particularly bad headache plagues me, I don't mention it. I smile through the pain and I never complain. I'm helpful, pleasant and obedient, trying to be seen and not heard. I will give them no ammunition.

I've been spending as much time outside as I can, away from prying eyes. Early winter here is relatively mild, for the most part. The snow tends not to accumulate, and melts quickly as it falls. I walk laps around the house, counting my steps – it soothes and comforts me.

On this particular morning, I round the East side of the mansion leading to the garden; a trellis now covered in dead ivy marking it's entrance. Aloysius, as usual, goes about his work, come snow or shine. He knows I'm there, but he pays me no mind, being compelled to tend to his flowers, even though they have long since frozen and died, and are black with decay. He busies himself with repetitive, unnecessary tasks, like he is unaware of their uselessness. It's sad really. He's not at peace, he can't be, but he's harmless.

Harmless that is, until the unexpected happens, and I finally make the connection between the gentle innocuous ghosts, like Aloysius and the wicked hurtful beings they turn into, like Clara and Henry.

As Aloysius works unaware, a black figure perches on the top of the glass greenhouse above him. A gaping, spiteful smile distorts his otherwise featureless face. As I watch, unable to look away, he climbs down from the little building, standing beside Aloysius, so close they begin to meld, overlapping and blurring together.

It is then that Aloysius, the most inconspicuous and unassuming of all the spirits comes charging at me, garden shears raised menacingly in his hand, his face a mask of fury. I start to run, faster than I've ever ran before. Aloysius follows, and as I reach the edge of the garden, he lunges at me, fading away before he drives his shears into my back. Just like that he's gone. He can't go any farther than the garden, I realize that, but he's never threatened my life before. I collapse to the ground trying to catch my breath, panting and heaving. What the staff must think if they are watching me through the windows now, because only I can see the black figure crawl back up to his perch on the greenhouse roof, taking his place like a sentry on duty.

It all makes sense now. The black figures, the shadow people, the ones that hide in corners of the house and behind doors, throwing books at Miss Millie and ripping Uncle's painting off the wall - they are obviously the cause of Clara, Henry, Aloysius and no doubt Simon's transformation from amicable to vengeful and fiendish. I've just seen it with my own two eyes. But where did the demons come from? How did a houseful of peaceful ghosts, likely for centuries, become invaded by such a sinister force? If only there was an answer to that mystery, the house could return to harmony – the living and the dead co-existing together, in their own realms without fear and violence. If this were so, then I too could find peace.

xii:

After dinner, I know what I must do. While the staff is cleaning up after the evening meal, I head to Uncle's office. Praying he has some answers, some explanation for what has turned this house sour, I tentatively knock on his door. He opens it momentarily, arched brows indicating he's surprised to see me.

"Well, how are you doing, Adelia? Are you feeling better these days?"

He invites me in and encourages me to sit on the settee,

giving me his undivided attention. I smile. He's a good Uncle...how could I ever doubt his intentions?

"I need to ask you some questions, for my own peace of mind. I hope you don't think them strange." I look away, fingers fidgeting, suddenly shy and self conscious.

"Why of course, ask anything you like." He clasps his hands together, his eyes never leaving mine.

I want to choose my words carefully, to avoid causing him concern, but in the end, I just end up blurting out, "Have there ever been any murders in this house?"

In my mind, that would explain it all; an event that invited in the presence of evil, shattering the calm, altering the tranquility of the afterlife.

He looks at me oddly, shaking his head. "No, not that I know of. Over the years, people have died here yes, accidents, old age, suicide even, as you know. But no one has ever been killed by those means. Nothing so horrible has ever happened here. Tell me child, why do you ask?"

I answer his question with another question. I need to get it all out before fear stops me.

"Uncle, has there ever been any seances here? Has anyone ever practiced the black arts, used a spirit board, tried to summon spirits?" I look up at him anxiously.

He sits back, alarmed, almost offended.

"Of course not. This family has always had an upstanding reputation in this town. Nothing of that sort has or would have ever happened here. If anything, my relatives were always the superstitious sort. They never would have participated in anything that questionable, that wasn't totally above board. Now why do you ask?"

I'm at a loss for words.

Uncle Lewis sighs, hanging his head, and for a moment he says nothing. I fear I have gone too far. When he looks up again, his eyes look weary, his face defeated.

"My dear girl, I can only assume this is about those ghosts you always tell me you see. The only reason that might ring with even the remotest truth, is that you, like Twyla, like Henry, might be blessed with the gift of sight, as we discussed before. Now it's time to tell you why that gift can be a curse," he begins, but I interrupt.

"It is certainly a curse Uncle, in fact..."

He put his hand up, shushing me.

"It is a curse to those around you, dear child."

I'm taken aback, immediately becoming silent.

"Henry used to scare us terribly with his experiences. We never could tell if what he truly believed was a product of his mental illness or not. It's sad to say, but when he died, the relief was palpable. Nothing odd happened, the air in the house was just different, as though he took it all with him when he left; all the madness, all the mystery."

I digested his words, "But Twyla also saw things that

frightened her. You told me so.”

“Twyla spun many tales in her day. When she lived with us, she was constantly telling your father and I stories, terrible stories, ghost stories... graphic details about everything she saw in and around the house. I think she embellished and made things up, but when you're a child, well, it sticks in your mind. It bothered your father most of all, he being the youngest. Her tales terrified him. He was unable to sleep; he became anxious and afraid of everything.” He paused, sitting down at his desk, twirling his pencil in his fingers, “When Twyla fled the house, it was once again calm. She took all her negativity with her also, much to our relief. Life was back to normal.”

“Did Twyla hear the ghosts too? Did they tell her to do terrible things?” I was on the edge of my seat, looking at him in anticipation.

He cocks his head, “Tell her to do terrible things? Not that I'm aware of. But then again, I was young.”

He pauses and sits forward.

"Are the ghosts telling you to do terrible things, Adelia?"

Now he looks concerned.

He says my name once more to get my attention, because I'm no longer looking at him. A dark figure stands just behind him, looking at me with sightless eyes. What it wants me to do is reprehensible, and for Uncle Lewis' safety I flee the room without another word. As I run through the door, I look back over my shoulder. The dark figure has climbed back behind the heavy drapes and Uncle watches me leave, with a pained expression on his face.

I race up the winding staircase. I used to love the pillars at the bottom, carved into cherubs, leading the way up to the second floor, but now they look angry and accusing as I pass. When I get to my room, I slam the door shut and lock it behind me, leaning against it to catch my breath. Breathing heavily, I don't hear it at first...but my breath soon catches in my throat.

Scratching...from under the bed...from inside the closet. Groans of anguish...snarls of anger. It's surrounds me, I can't get away from it.

I sink to the floor, back against the door. Shuddering uncontrollably, I watch in horror as a grey, corpse-like hand pushes open the closet door. Henry creeps out, noose dangling around his neck, crawling towards me. Clara is trying to get out from under my bed, one hand after the other slapping on the ground, her long fingernails scratching at the wooden floor, as pulls herself out. Her bloodstained dress slides across the floor as they both converge upon me. They're angry at me. I'm not doing as they please, not complying with their wishes...and right now what they want me to do is kill Uncle Lewis.

I could go back downstairs, quietly sneak back into his office, pick up the shiny silver letter opener on his desk and stab him. Or I could go to the kitchen and steal some of the rat poison kept under the sink and put it in his coffee. I could always call him up to my room and be waiting at the top of the stairs to push him down. So many ways to kill Uncle Lewis...breathing heavy, a wry smile spreads upon my face – until I catch myself.

No!

I won't!

But I'm feeling so powerless. My resolve is weakening.
I've been fighting for so long, against the evil that
threatens to take over. I managed to overcome it once,
with Jonathan, but I'm not sure if I'm strong enough to do
it again. I feel the vile, foul beings becoming more and
more malignant; their intentions are diabolical and
heinous. I'm losing myself in them...I'm fading away and
being absorbed by their energy.

Clara and Henry stare at me...they want me just to give
up...succumb to them..and I'm tired, so very tired...

So, it takes every ounce of fortitude I have, to push myself
off the ground and run out of that room, slamming the
door behind me. And I don't stop running until I'm outside
and down the road, out of sight of the house. Only when it
is no longer looming behind me, do I stop, bending over,

gasping for air.

The sun is beginning to slowly sink into the woods, marking the end of the day. The twilight sky is full of brilliant pinks, oranges and blues, much like a prism. All too soon it will be replaced by shades of black, but I need to go to the accident site one more time. I need to see my parents, ask them so many questions, beg of them why did they leave me here alone.

I'm not wearing a coat. The air is biting cold, and each breath shows as a plume of white steam. I wrap my arms around myself as I walk slowly, but with purpose. I reach the rock and take my place. After last time, being forced to re-live the car accident over and over again, I've been hesitant to come back here. I'm shivering as I sit and wait, but I don't know whether it's from the cold or my nerves.

Before I'm ready, my parents appear in the distance. As they walk towards me, it pains me to see their appearance. Their decomposition is evident; mottled, rotting skin beginning to slough off, eyes sunken deeply in their skulls. But yet, they still smile.

I stand up and they stop walking, standing twenty feet in front of me.

"Oh mother, father, please help me! Tell me what I should do. Tell me what is happening. I feel like I'm going crazy." I begin to cry, wanting nothing more than a mother's embrace, but knowing it will never be so.

I sit back down, hands covering my eyes as I sob at the hopelessness of it all, at the insanity of it all; mourning my my losses. The wind whispers in my ear and I feel a touch on my shoulder. Mother is in front of me, as she was before the accident, beautiful and perfect. She holds out her hand to and I take it, feeling her hand firmly in mine. Unsure what is happening, but not wanting it to end, I stand up and let her lead me towards my father. He's standing beside the idling black sedan that I spent so many days in while we travelled here - the sedan that I last saw as a twisted piece of metal, crushed beyond recognition. But here it sits, just as it was, as though I've travelled back in time. She opens the back door and I get in, sliding onto the firm leather seats.

The car smells of sandalwood and my father's cologne. He sits in the driver's seat and turns around, winking at me with the handsome smile I remember so well, lighting up a cigar. I want to say so much, ask so many questions, but I can't speak. I can only be here in this moment with them, and hope it never ends.

It is dusk and we're heading towards the Estate. I remember being impatient to get there, tired of sitting in the car for so many, many miles. It was such a long trip across the country to see his brother, whom he hadn't seen in years. He never explained the reason for the trip. It is playing out, just as it did that night. I am powerless to stop it, but I need answers.

I close my eyes, as I did that night, but I'm not sleeping, only dozing, as my mother sings along to a song on the radio. Her voice is melodic and hypnotizing, relaxing me into a light sleep. That is until they start arguing. Mother looks into the back to check that I'm sleeping and I keep my eyes closed. She turns back to my father. They are trying to be quiet, but I hear them – I hear every word.

"I'm not sure we're doing the best thing." She sighs.

"Don't start this again." His voice is short and curt.

"I don't know why you insisted on coming all the way here. You haven't been here in years…"

Before she can continue, he interrupts her, "There is nowhere else close to us. I've explained that to you time and time again. We should be grateful to have found a place which is so near my family, so we have a place to stay, so we can visit whenever we want."

"Your family that you haven't seen in years." She scoffs.

"My family history is my business. Can we please stay focused on why we are making this trip? This is for Adelia. That's why we're doing this. We're getting her the help she needs." His voice is sure and firm, as he puffs on his cigar.

My eyes fly open. Never once did they mention this trip

was for me, or about me. I was under the impression that we were simply visiting his long lost family. My mind starts racing. What is happening? Closing my eyes again, I remain quiet. If they realize I'm listening, they'll stop talking.

"She needs help, Annabelle. We agreed on that long ago."

My heart beats so quickly, I fear they can hear it in the silence between their words.

"I know, Miles. I know." Her voice is soft, fragile, like it could break at any moment.

"We should have done this sooner. When she first started talking about seeing things, hearing things..."

"I thought it was just an imaginary friend. I so wanted it to be." Her voice cracks and catches in her throat. She's crying softly now.

"She's going to get the help she needs. We are doing the right thing. This hospital is the best in the country. We are lucky they've agreed to take her." His voice is brusque. He sounds impatient, like he's been through this with her a thousand times before.

A sharp pain travels through my head, a pain like no other, zinging and zapping it's way around my brain until synapses begin making connections that had been lost since the accident...and I remember. I remember everything.

Our last night as a family plays out moment by moment just as it did the first time all those months ago, and finally I remember exactly how it all happened.

I know what's coming next. I'm afraid to open my eyes, but I'm compelled to do so. In the seat beside me sits the black figure, leaning towards me, his face far too close to mine. He's smiling at me, head cocked; a mocking, terrifying smile.

As I did back then, I scream, an ear splitting, high pitched wail that resonates throughout the car. I bolt upright and lunge forward, grabbing the front seat. Everyone is yelling; the car closes in around me. I feel like a caged animal; I can't seem to get enough air. My parents are startled. Mother is trying in vain to calm me down, her face full of panic and fear. The car veers to the other side of the road, but my father manages to wrestle it back in line. He rolls down the window and angrily throws out his cigar, looking at me in the rear view mirror with exasperation.

With crystal clarity, a movie plays in my head. All the memories come flooding back at once...

From the moment I was old enough to speak, I began talking about the black figures I'd see around me. They would hide in my room, coming out of the shadows when I tried to sleep, whispering unintelligible things in my ear. They would lurk behind the big grandfather clock that stood in the living room or peek through the windows.

Oh I was terrified at first, I thought our house was haunted. But it became apparent that I was the only one who could see them. Inexplicably, they were only attached to me. I would catch a glimpse of them out of the corner of my eye no matter where I was. These were not friendly spirits of dear, departed loves ones... there was something very sinister about them. Even so, they were for the most part harmless, even if they would often throw or break things I would get blamed for.

I begged my parents to understand, but they brushed it off as imaginary playmates. They didn't know what to do, so for the longest time they did nothing. But I continued to talk about it; I told everyone. I would embarrass my parents by talking about it in mixed company, at the shops, at church. At school, I would upset my friends, pointing out a figure standing behind them that only I could see. They didn't believe me, but I frightened them. I became an outcast, the strange child that no one wanted to be friends with. And that just made it all the worse, because the lonelier I became, the tighter the demons clung to me. No one else could ever see them. Confusion, fear and frustration changed me. I never was quite right, but I was only trying to cope however I could.

And so, on that evening in the Spring, we were finishing the last leg of the journey from our home hours and miles away to the finest hospital for the mentally ill. My father didn't know what else to do for me and was advised by our own doctor that I'd best be put away, like all feeble-minded or crazy relatives are...that's just what you do in this day and age. They saw no other choice, but I am deeply wounded nonetheless that they would dare do that to me.

I want to protest, to beg for mercy, but something catches my eye. Out the front window, in the middle of the road, stands a towering black figure, and father is driving straight towards it. I point and screech, pulling frantically at my father's arm from the backseat.

"See it! Please! See it!" I yell in his ear.

Mother is trying to pull me off him, but I hang on to his neck, his rough whiskers scratching my skin. He loses control and the car hits the shoulder, beginning a death roll like an alligator with its prey. It happens so fast, yet it happens in slow motion. I am tossed around the car as it topples. The sounds of glass breaking and screaming, no doubt including my own, echoes in my ears. When the car finally comes to rest, it is upside down. The chaos ends as quickly as it began It is suddenly dark and quiet. My parents are completely silent, mangled in the twisted wreck, their bodies bent at impossible angles. Our blood conjoins and pools beneath me, as I lay on the ceiling on a bed of broken glass, In and out of consciousness, I open my eyes briefly, as someone, a passerby I suppose, pulls me from the vehicle. The wheels of the car spin towards the sky. The strong smell of gas burns my nose. Plumes of smoke rise from the undercarriage and just as we get far enough away, it explodes. My eyes close and don't open for a long time.

Uncle Lewis had told me I was in a coma for several weeks; it was uncertain if I would live, then uncertain if I would ever wake up. Miraculously, I did and Uncle Lewis was at my bedside. As my only living relative on this side of the country, he felt it was his duty to take me in, now that I was left an orphan.

I can only assume he didn't know the reason behind our trip. Perhaps he only knew that he was soon to be reunited with his brother after many years of estrangement. If my father had told him the reason we were coming, he chose never to follow through with the plans to send me to the hospital. Given the family history, maybe he knew I wasn't crazy after all; just the victim of the family curse, so to speak. But he couldn't have imagined the evil I was bringing with me.

xiii:

The painful realization that I caused the accident leaves me devastated...shocked. I am an orphan of my own doing. I can no longer think straight. Grief stricken and overwhelmed with guilt, my mind fractures in a bazillion pieces.

I wake up lying on the ground in the exact place the car landed - the very spot where I was laying on the ceiling of when it came to rest after rolling over and over for what seemed like an eternity. The accident scene is clear, my parents are gone. The frosty winter air has seeped into my bones. I don't know how long I've been laying here. But I don't feel the cold, I don't feel anything.

The full moon lights my way back towards Craymore Estate. The fresh fallen snow gleams beneath my feet. I trudge through it, ruining the flawless ground cover with my footprints.

I feel like I'm walking through molasses, each foot an effort to lift up and back down. My mind is blank, there are no emotions, no feelings, just numbness. Frost has settled on my hair, my eyelashes stick each time I blink.

The world is white and quiet like static. Being all alone in the silence makes me wonder if I too, actually perished in the crash. Am I dead or am I alive? I'm not even sure. I just keep walking, one foot in front of the other, until the Estate comes into view. It beckons me home, and at the same time it dares me to come back. It taunts me, it lures me..it wants me to run and never look back.

In the woods beyond, I see lights and I know Uncle and his staff must be searching for me. Three lanterns bob up and down in the distance, and as I get closer, I can faintly hear them calling my name. I don't answer.

I continue on around the back of the house until I reach the pond. I expect to see Simon brightly illuminated in the light of the moon, but he doesn't seem to be there. The moon dances on the water as I stop and look around. In the distance, his head breaks the surface and his arms are flailing. He's splashing and sinking, only to reappear again, the water rippling around him. I can hear him frantically sputtering and trying to yell for help, but he sounds like he's tiring. He's drowning and dying, just as he did all those years ago. Why am I being shown such heartbreak?

I run into the pond to help him, to save him. The bitter icy, water shocks me. My leg muscles seize and cramp almost instantly, and I'm unable to get any farther. Disappearing below the surface for the last time, the air bubbles come to a stop. I've failed him. Standing in the water up to my waist, I've now taken Simon's place in the pond. I turn around and look at the house, the view that Simon has had every day. At my bedroom window in the turret, I see Henry and Clara gazing down at me.

Sensing something behind me, I turn around slowly.

Simon is there again, standing stoically in the water, as he was always, as he always will be...as though he didn't just die all over again. His pale skin seems to glow in the moonlight. History seems doomed to repeat itself, so before it begins again, I must leave. I don't want to watch him drown over and over, just as I have already experienced the tragic car accident time and time again.

Henry and Clara's pull is strong and I'm drawn back to the house. Now soaking wet in the frigid air, I still don't feel the cold. No longer hearing the calls of Uncle and the staff looking for me in the woods, I trudge a path back to the house, entering through the servants quarters in the back.

The house is very bright, every room lit with an oil lamp. They must have searched the entire house for me before venturing out into the raw winter night. How worried Uncle must be, his staff dutifully by his side. Maybe he's searching for a ghost that never existed to begin with. Maybe he's searching for a demon he doesn't want to find. Or maybe he's just searching for a lost little girl who's soul has been stolen, it's flame snuffed out by whatever ungodliness pursues this family. None of it matters anymore.

The cherubs at the bottom of the grand staircase turn their heads and smile menacingly as I walk between them. With one hand on the baluster, my fingernails scratch a trail in the fine wood all the way up. The paintings of my ancestors on the wall follow me with their eyes, watching me, always watching... I fear they will reach out and grab me, but they remain still. I think I hear them whispering...

Pushing open the door to my room, I enter the past...as it was back then. My small bed by the window is gone, replaced by a large canopy bed, garishly baroque, but at the same time elegantly beautiful and detailed, sitting right beside the doorway. I run my hand over the rich fabric pillows. The room smells of jasmine, lit dimly by candles on every surface. The only thing I recognize as mine is the vanity, sitting where it always has, but now full of perfumes and tonics, hairbrushes and jewellery.

Where my bed used to be stands a huge armoire, consisting of three different sections, handcrafted with intricate details carved into the doors. Varnished and lacquered to a sheen, it is obviously made of the finest mahogany that money could buy. It is a wealthy person's dream wardrobe, the focal point of the room.

Clara is dwarfed by the piece. My eyes settle on her as she is standing on her tip toes, reaching for a box that is sitting on the top. In life, she was a small woman, frail as she aged. But here she is, dressed in her finest clothes, determined to reach whatever it is in that box. She's frustrated by her inability to get it, becoming impatient. She can see it, touch it, but it is caught on the lip. There's nothing for her to stand on to give her the height she needs. I want to help her, but I'm rooted to the spot and I'm not in her world...not really anyway. History has merely opened it doors, making me watch as it all unfolds.

She grabs the corner of the lid and she pulls, hoping it will slide over the top. The armoire is not secured to the wall; it stands freely on four small, curved feet. As she tugs it begins to move, gently banging against the wall. But she is undeterred and stretches as tall as she can muster, getting a good grip on the corner of the box lid. What could be so important, that would cause her reckless disregard for her own safety? She's tiring with the effort, but gives a final good tug on the box. The huge wooden wardrobe teeters and falls forward, coming down hard on top of her, pinning her to the floor with a bang. The wind is knocked out of her and she let's out a cry of pain. A small pool of blood seeps from underneath, but she is still alive, she has survived the initial accident. But her family has not returned from the city, having been gone for hours to celebrate the opening of another new business they've funded. They are not due back for many hours yet. Thanks to some shrewd business minds before them, their wealth and prestige is increasing every day, but that cannot save the tragedy that has befallen Clara.

As I watch, time passes in an instant. Clara lays on that floor, the armoire slowly crushing her chest, unable to get enough air for hours and hours. She's a strong woman, but she's aged and hasn't much fight left in her. The small pool of blood beneath her grows steadily larger, perhaps from a head injury or maybe internal bleeding. Her arm sticks out from underneath, constantly moving and twitching, until it finally becomes still. She is gone. What

a horrible fate she suffered. What a horrible way to die,
slowly and alone, feeling the life seep out of her. I'm sorry
Clara, you didn't deserve this.

What is so important that Clara needed so badly from the
top of that wardrobe? The box has fallen, opening and
spilling it's contents. I creep quietly over and kneel down
beside the overturned armoire. The box looks familiar,
I've seen it before... it contains pictures. I pick them up
and look at them, they are the same pictures I came across
in the attic buried deep within the trunk - the pictures of
family members who had passed away and the memento
mori photos of the generations before. I've looked at all of
these pictures before. In fact, Clara's would also be added
to the collection later on. The people in the photos have
morphed and transformed – the faces are twisted and
angry, with malicious grins and wrathful grimaces. The
photos of the dead, like their spirits, are warped and
without peace. Snarling mouths and glaring, accusing eyes
stare back at me. I drop them, as though they are hot as
fire, and then I realize what Clara was trying to do.

Beside her on a small table are several long fireplace

matches and a metal ash bucket. She was planning to burn the photos, just like Henry had tried to do. They were, no doubt, terrorizing and haunting her and she just wanted to turn them to ashes, to stop the horror, to escape the family history in which she also became ensnared.

Poor Clara. In life she was a mother, a wife, a human being with feelings, compassion and love. But because of the unholy demons that haunt this family, death has transformed her into an unrecognizable monster. Even though I deeply regret that I brought evil with me when I came to Craymore Manor, it is impossible to know how many others who were here before me embodied it also. The house contained the powder keg and the spark already, I just threw more fuel on the fire.

Why the blackness only attaches to some of us, only terrorizes some of us, is a mystery that I fear will never be solved. It is impossible to get answers, because those who are unaffected, like Uncle Lewis, can't understand and don't believe. They turn a blind eye to that which they can't comprehend, but the fact remains, someone invited evil into this family. Somehow a door was open that can't be closed. Lord help us all.

The faintest of sounds reaches my ear – people talking. Running to the bedroom window, I see Uncle, the butler and Miss Millie below. They are heading around the house up the front drive, presumably to search for me along the road and the woods on either side. Uncle turns to look up at the house and I duck behind the curtain. He mustn't see me. He can't know what I've become. It's not safe for him to be near me, not when the evil commands me so. I'm only thinking of him. He was kind enough to take over my care. Of course, it was simply out of familial obligation, but he did it nonetheless. He could have turned me over to the orphanage or the hospital, but family is important to him, as is legacy and heritage. So much so that he watches over this house, the keeper of the phantoms and revenants, without even being aware of his importance. His presence here is fundamental to their existence, their permanence. What would become of them if he left the property, or if the property was destroyed? What will become of them when he passes on? Or if something terrible were to befall him when he returns to the house tonight? They will need a new Gatekeeper.

I watch until their lantern lights disappear in the distance, so far away that they resemble little dancing fireflies, and eventually fade away all together. Opening my bedroom window wide, I breathe in the cold night air, looking to the heavens. A brisk wind rushes into the room, making the curtains flutter; my long hair twists around my face. Stepping up onto the wide windowsill, I pull the window up, opening it as far as it will go. I can almost stand tall, but need to crouch slightly to avoid banging my head. How easy it would be to jump right now, to let myself fall to the ground below. I lean out and look down. I would either land in the rock garden, or if I leapt, I might land on the wrought iron fence, impaling myself on the spear like post caps. The only thing stopping me is the fear of the ground opening up and swallowing me into Hell below. That's probably where I belong anyway, given this wicked, wicked mind...given the compulsions and impulses bestowed upon me by the devil himself. Behind me, Clara whispers for me to jump, begs me to jump...

That's when I hear Henry, and he's the only thing that pulls me off that ledge, for when I turn around, the room has transformed itself once again. It is no longer Clara's femininely decorated boudoir, it is now sparsely adorned; just a single bed, a desk and chair, and a tall dresser. There are no pictures on the wall, nothing that makes it looked lived in; minimalist at best. It is Henry's room now, and I see him busying himself in front of the closet. His back is to me, but when he turns slightly, I can see that he's knotting a thick rope in his hands. He sniffles once, wipes his eyes with the back of his hand, then quickly sets back to work. When he's satisfied that his rope is strong, he opens the closet door. Then he turns around and looks at me with wide eyes, pupils flared. Many emotions fly across his face, but then his mouth twitches slightly, curving into a grotesque smile, eyes narrowing and burning with rage.

I can't look away, my eyes are glued to his every move. Henry's closet contains only the fewest of clothes: three similar white button down shirts and two pairs of black trousers. He is a simple man, his needs are few and his wants even fewer. He was not interested in material things, as he lived very much inside his head, making him susceptible, you see. They prey on the weak minded, the introspective, it seems. He pushes the clothes aside and drapes the end of the rope over the thick iron bar, securing it tightly, his eyes never leaving mine.

Slipping the noose over his head, he pulls it taut. I begin to shake my head, slowly at first, then more vigorously.

"Don't....."

Before I can get the words out, he falls to his knees. The rope becomes rigid and tense. He could so easily avoid his demise buy simply getting to his feet, but it's obvious what his end goal is. His face quickly becomes red, then purple. He sinks slowly into the corner, gurgling noises and gasps for air coming from his strangled throat, until his tongue begins to protrude and his face turns a deep purple. His eyes are wide and his limbs tremor, as the purple fades into a sickly blue. And all the while, he eyes on are me. He dies with them open, staring daggers at me.

xiv:

My room is my own again. Gone are any traces of Henry

or Clara's years of life here. Although it's not really my room. It belongs to family, to the generations before. I never belonged here; I wasn't accepted here, not by the living, nor the dead.

Henry and Clara are quiet...for now...their needs satiated for the time being by the glorious displays of their deaths. Simon stands in the pond beyond the house, in his proper place, standing on guard. All is as it should be, but it is my turn to be restless. Uncle and the staff are still out combing the road and woods for any sign of me. I don't know how much time has passed. But I do know one thing. Before crawling back under the bed, her eternal resting place, Clara whispered something in my ear.

And she's right.

She's so very right.

Sighing, I leave the bedroom. Slowly down the grand staircase, resolute in mind and body, I run my fingernails down the wall, leaving gouges in the rich, flowered wallpaper as I go. The framed black and white photographs of the ancestors, none of whom I've met, stare at me, judging me, accusing me, loathing me. They are the faces of those gone long before me. I wonder what secrets they took to the grave with them. I wonder how many of them came back.

As I pass by, without turning my head to look at them, I swipe each frame off the wall, one after the other.

Crash...crash...crash.

Glass shatters around my feet, a bed of shards on the stairs. The frames bounce down the stairs, some of the pictures falling out and floating off in different directions, some straight down to the ground. I step on them and keep walking to the bottom landing. The cherubs are smiling sweetly, heads turned upwards, gazing at me warmly. Sickeningly sweet smiles belie rage filled eyes. Despite their upturned lips, the eyes stare right into my soul with indignation and hate.

I know what I must do. For myself. For all of them.

The house remains brightly lit, and I can see the evidence of the frantic search that was conducted – coats and boxes pulled out of closets, blankets and pillows from the sofas and chairs lay strewn on the floor. I enter Uncle's office first. The fireplace there smoulders down to it's last coals with no one there to stoke it. It is becoming damp, and I am still so wet from the pond.

I walk past the sitting room and the library and enter Uncle's office. His large wooden desk is covered in books, and papers. Ink drips from his fountain pen, onto some ledgers, looking as though it was thrown there haphazardly. He must have been dipping it into the inkwell when he was called by Miss Millie perhaps, noticing I was gone.

Looking around the room, I gaze at the paintings on the walls, scenes of landscapes and buildings, mountains and forests. Curiously, there are no pictures of people here. No photographs of relatives adorn the walls or sit on the shelves. No pictures of his parents or his brother. Uncle created a space for himself where he didn't have any faces staring back at him. He surrounded himself with places, where he could get lost, escape the family history. Maybe that's why he spent so much time here. It was his refuge away from human beings, where he could be alone with his thoughts, knowing that outside the office door was reality that he couldn't change or ignore. Perhaps he knew he was tethered to this house in life, as much as the others were in death. Or maybe, just maybe, Uncle was never alive after all. Maybe that's why he remained so steadfastly in this house, in this office. Could it be? Nothing makes sense anymore. I don't know who is alive and who is dead. I don't know which I am either.

My head hurts.

It hurts so much.

I take a moment to rest, leaning against his desk, closing my eyes and touching my fingertips to my temples. My hand finds the oil lamp sitting on the corner near me, and I knock it off the desk with a casual swipe of my hand, not unlike a naughty cat. But the cat is really not naughty after all, is it? It's just following its nature, its instinct... just as I am following Clara's.

The lamp crashes to the parquet floor and the sickly sweet smell of kerosene fills my nose, fills the room. I open my eyes when I feel the hot glow lick my ankles and watch the flames dance across the floor, the wood easily catching alight and spreading. How tempting it is just to stand in place and go up in a pyre. But I have things to do.

Leaving the fire to do its bidding, I walk out of the office, down the long hall and into the large dining room at the back of the house. This room signifies loneliness to me, as I always ate my meals alone here, surrounded by strangers who weren't interested in being my friends. This room also signifies silence to me, as the only noises were the clinking of my cutlery on the finest bone china.

The long dining table, heavy and wooden, has a crisp white table cloth with a beautiful red velvet runner laying on it, adorned with a large seasonal centrepiece in the middle, accented with pine boughs and birch sticks. Miss Millie is beginning her Christmas decor it seems. On either side sit several oil lamps of different sizes, giving the room a warm glow. I walk around the table, knocking each lamp off with a crash. The table cloth catches fire quickly and the centrepiece goes up in a loud whoosh, flames shooting towards the chandelier above. I watch in fascination, as the fire frolics around the room in a frenzied choreography. It's beautiful really. Pirouetting and twirling, like partners waltzing in each other's arms. It's time to go. I leave them to their recital, turning my back on the destruction, and head back up the hall.

The sitting room is one of formal elegance. In this room, I can picture the polite company and socializing of yore. Women in corsets and fascinators sit quietly but primly with fine tea cups between their thumbs and forefingers, pinkies in the air as their class dictates, while distinguished men in top hats and suits talk business. Many informal meetings were held here. Many family members lounged on the cabriole sofa with it's pretty bowed legs, or on the tufted chaise in the corner. If only these pieces of furniture could tell their tales, what stories I would hear. But alas, the walls already talk too much.

Oil lamps sit brightly lit on the mantle piece and on the side tables. I swipe them onto the floor too, in quick succession.

Crash...crash...crash...

I walk out before seeing what will become of them. The
smell of kerosene is now quite strong and I welcome the
sweet burn. The house is alive with crackling and hissing,
and the flaring whooshes around me. It is as much noise,
as I've ever heard since I've been here. Normally the only
din is the murmur of the staff, as they do their jobs quietly
and effectively. The house is waking up, stretching and
yawning...groaning and moaning...growling and popping.
It makes me smile. I turn my head to look as I walk past
the wall mirror in the hall. The smile on my face is not
my own. It is contorted, with bared teeth... and dead,
unblinking eyes. I don't recognize that face. Who is that?
It doesn't matter.

On to the library, arguably my favourite room. Books
stacked from floor to ceiling on wall to wall shelves that
require an attached sliding ladder to access. Many an hour
I spent here, trying to lose myself in someone else's story,
for mine was undesirable. The oversized chair and sofa

were the perfect place to escape for just awhile. I run my hand over the soft, rich fabric as I head to the oil lamp that sits on the windowsill, knocking it over with a firm hand. Standing in the doorway, I watch as all the beautiful books burn, going up in an instant. So flammable. So pretty.

Back in the hallway now, I can see each room behind me lit up with flickering flames, fire eating everything in its path. Out the doorways, it travels, into the hall beginning its slow crawl towards me, devouring as it goes.

And I let it follow behind me, as I go from room to room finishing my task. Then I go back up the grand staircase, not bothering to acknowledge the cherubs, they will burn soon anyway. They won't be a bother any longer.

At the top of the stairs, I take a moment to look over the railing to the floor below and survey my work. Clara will be proud. The whole bottom story has come alive with oranges, reds and yellows. Like Autumn itself dancing along, travelling towards me.

The pictures are sure to burn now, Clara. I will finish

what you and Henry had tried to do. They needed to burn...and so they will. It will all burn. It is all for the best. It's the only way to stop it all. Release all the souls and the demons will be forced to leave too. I release you all. I am the new Gatekeeper.

Perhaps this is all a dream? I don't know what's real and what's not anymore. It doesn't matter, really. The fire is rushing up the stairs, and I can feel the heat as it travels towards me. The top floor is quickly becoming engulfed as I go back into my bedroom, leaving the door open.

I hear shouting, faintly in the distance and look out the window. Lantern lights far down the road bounce up and down quickly, getting closer, as Uncle and the staff are running towards the house. It went up like a tinderbox, after all. How glorious it must look from the outside.

And now, suddenly, I tire.

And I'm cold. So very cold.

I feel the dead of winter in my bones. Crawling into bed, I lay my weary head on the pillow and pull the blanket up to my chin. I'm shivering, but I'll be warm soon.

It's time to rest.

Epilogue

My parents always used to say, 'There is no change without sacrifice'. I let it go in one ear and out the other, but now I realize just how poignant those words can be.

There are many different kinds of sacrifices – some good and some, well some that come at quite a cost. In the moment, I couldn't comprehend my actions or the consequences of them, but in the end I can only hope that it has freed this plagued and tortured family.

My eyes flutter open. The sky is the most purest blue I've ever seen. I'm standing on the back lawn, facing the pond. Simon is no longer there. He's running towards me, a big smile on his face. When he reaches me, he is beaming from ear to ear. How handsome he looks with his hair combed just so, wearing a button down shirt and dungarees. And he's so thankful to be released from his watery prison.

Underneath a grove of trees in the distance stands Henry and Clara, conversing quietly. They look over and wave politely, beckoning me to join them. Aloysius wanders over to them, acknowledging me with a polite nod. They are not aware of what became of them since their deaths. Their journey to the spirit world was interrupted; they were hostages between the realms of the living and the dead. I am the only one who knows the truth of it all...and I have released them. I am the Gatekeeper.

Behind me, Uncle Lewis walks amongst the charred ruins of his beloved, yet cursed family home. There are tears in his eyes. I like to think they're for me and not just the Estate. I want to run over and hug him, even though his reaction would be stiff and uncomfortable; he is not used to shows of affection, you see. I wish I could tell him I'm alright but he won't see me...he'll never see me...

The house continues to smoulder, plumes of wispy smoke

rising into the air. I like to think it's souls escaping; that thought makes me smile. The house burned to the ground, in a fire hotter than Hell itself. It can never be salvaged. It will never again hold the dead...or the living. Uncle Lewis is now also freed from a prison of his own making. He will go on to achieve great things with other like minds. Isolation was not becoming, nor healthy for him. He'll be just fine; he just needs some time to process everything. Maybe one day, he'll believe...but if he never does, that's alright too. It's enough that I know all the secrets. I wouldn't want him to be burdened with such things anyway.

Looking around at my new surroundings, I smile and take a deep breath, feeling more like myself than I ever have since the accident. We will all exist peacefully here now. There is only one thing missing.

I run around to the front yard and stand at the beginning of the long driveway. Shading my eyes with my hand, I squint and crane my neck, waiting and watching.

My face lights up when I see them walking towards the

house. My father and mother, hand in hand, strolling towards me with smiles on their faces. Handsome and beautiful as they were in life; untouched by the ravages of death. We can finally be together again. What a sweet reunion it will be.

But then, in an instant the world turns upside down. As quick as a heartbeat, everything has changed. Icy dread slams into the pit of my stomach and a feeling of hopelessness blacker than midnight washes over me. A look of horror spreads across my face as I watch my parents approach one step at a time.

In the distance behind them, an all too familiar dark figure follows...

THE END